paris fling

A BWWM Forced Family Romance

dylan roxi

Paris Fling
Copyright © 2025 by Dylan Roxi
All rights reserved.

Book Cover and formatting provided by Trisha Fuentes
https://bit.ly/m/trishafuentes

No part of this book may be reproduced in any form or by any electronic or mechanical means, including information storage and retrieval systems, without written permission from the author, except for the use of brief quotations in a book review.

ISBN: 979-8-3482-0270-5 (Paperback)

Published by
Ardent Artist Books
www.ardentartistbooks.com

about ardent artist books

➥ ABOUT US

Ardent Artist Books was established in 2008

We publish modern and historical romances once a month!

Get Your FREE List: Published & Upcoming Books
visit our website at:
https://bit.ly/3Wva4o0

* * *

➥ WE HAVE BOOK TRAILERS

Follow us on YouTube!
https://bit.ly/3W3xn7a

Like, Subscribe & Comment

* * *

➥ WE HAVE SERIALIZED FICTION!

Visit our website today to download one of our stories that unfold in bite-sized pieces!

Each installment is just 99¢!
Paperback $15.99

https://bit.ly/3LsDpJL

* * *

➥ LET'S CONNECT!

Fuel your love of fiction with exclusive content and captivating insights from Ardent Artist Books. Whether you crave the thrill of modern narratives or the timeless elegance of historical fiction, our newsletter delivers a curated selection straight to your inbox. Plus, as a welcome gift, receive a FREE downloadable eBook:

"The Family Fix"

https://bit.ly/49BR3UB

contents

1. The Call 1
2. ORD to CDG 11
3. An Evening in Montmartre 21
4. The Morning After 33
5. Parisian Café 41
6. The Dubois Residence 51
7. The Wedding Prep 61
8. Alexandre 69
9. Tanya 77
10. Limestone Steps 85
11. Au Revoir, Ma Belle 93
12. Back to Reality 103
13. Retour à la Normale 111
14. Epilogue 121

you might also like

Love Child - Part 1 131
Love Child - Part 2 133

new for 2025

Dorm Room 2B or Not 2B 137

About Dylan 139
Also by Dylan 141

the call
...
CHICAGO - Illinois

Tanya Washington's heels clicked against the polished concrete floor of her gallery as she directed the installation team. The afternoon sun streamed through the floor-to-ceiling windows, casting dramatic shadows across the vibrant canvases being mounted on pristine white walls.

"The lighting needs to hit Marcus's piece at exactly forty-five degrees." She gestured to the large abstract painting. "It's crucial for the texture to pop."

Her phone buzzed in her blazer pocket. Her mother's smiling face lit up the screen - their daily check-in right on schedule, like clockwork. Tanya smiled, their shared appreciation for punctuality one of the countless traits they had in common.

"I need to take this. Jake, make sure that sculpture is centered on the pedestal." She strode toward her office, already mentally reviewing their standing Sunday brunch plans.

The heavy glass door closed behind her with a soft click. She settled into her ergonomic chair and accepted the FaceTime call.

"Hey, Mama, I was thinking about trying that new Mexican place on Michigan Avenue when you get—"

"Baby girl!" Shaniece's face filled the screen, practically glowing. The background showed unfamiliar elegant architecture instead of her mother's Chicago office. "I have the most incredible news!"

Tanya's spine straightened. "Mama? Where are you?"

"Paris! And before you start worrying—I've met someone. The most amazing man. His name is Bernard François Dubois, and…" Shaniece's words tumbled out in an uncharacteristic rush, her usual corporate polish replaced by genuine excitement.

"Wait, what?" Tanya's fingers gripped her phone tighter. "You're in Paris? I thought you were at the London conference."

"I extended my trip. Bernard and I… we're engaged!"

The word hit Tanya like a physical blow. She forced her features to remain neutral even as her pulse quickened. "Engaged? What do you mean, you're engaged? Mama, you don't get engaged to someone you just met."

"When you know, you know. He's everything I never knew I was looking for," Shaniece's eyes sparkled. "We're planning the wedding for next month, here in Paris."

"Next month?" Tanya stood, pacing her office. "Mama, this isn't like you. You're the woman who spent three months researching coffee makers before buying one. You can't possibly know this man well enough to—"

"I know what I'm feeling, baby. For the first time in my life, I'm following my heart instead of my head."

"That's exactly what worries me," Tanya pinched the bridge of her nose. "Have you done any background checks? Asked about his finances? Met his family?"

"His family is wonderful. You'll see when you come to Paris."

"When I..." Tanya grabbed her tablet, fingers flying across the screen. "I'm booking a flight right now. We need to discuss this in person."

"Sweetheart, I know this seems sudden—"

"Sudden is a new hairstyle, Mama. This is..." Tanya found a direct flight leaving that evening. "I'll be there tomorrow morning. Send me your hotel details."

After ending the call, Tanya buzzed her assistant. "Cancel my appointments for the next week. Family emergency." She gathered her belongings, mind racing through logistics. "And Jake? Make sure those lighting adjustments get made exactly as specified."

The drive home was a blur of hands-free calls—arranging gallery coverage, updating her calendar, alerting her building's doorman. Her typically organized life had tilted sideways in the space of one conversation.

In her condo, Tanya threw open her closet doors and yanked her suitcase from the top shelf. Designer workwear and casual basics flew into the case with mechanical efficiency. A flash of black caught her eye—the cocktail dress her mother had given her last Christmas, price tags still attached.

Tanya smoothed the silk fabric of the cocktail dress, remembering how her mother's eyes had lit up when she'd picked it out. "Every woman needs that perfect little black dress," Shaniece had said, in the same tone she'd used to dispense wisdom throughout Tanya's life. The dress joined the neat rows of clothing in her suitcase, each piece selected with the same precision she applied to curating gallery exhibitions.

Bernard François Dubois.

Bernard François, sounded like a porn name...

Ugh... The name rolled around in her head like a marble in an empty jar. What happened to Marcus, the corporate attorney who'd been taking her mother to jazz clubs and wine tastings? The one who'd seemed so safe, so predictable, so... thoroughly vetted.

Her mother didn't do impulsive. Not since those early days when they'd shared a cramped one-bedroom apartment, and Shaniece had worked two jobs while studying for her marketing degree. Tanya remembered falling asleep to the sound of her mother's textbook pages turning ... the scratch of pen on paper as she prepared for exams.

She yanked open her jewelry box, selecting pieces that would transition from day to evening wear. The velvet-lined compartments reminded her of the cardboard shoe box where her mother used to keep their emergency fund—rolls of singles and fives from her waitressing tips, carefully counted each night after her shift.

"Sixteen with a baby," Shaniece would say, not with shame but as a statement of fact. "But that doesn't define who we become." She'd proved it too, climbing from entry-level marketing assistant to department head, then director, then VP. Each promotion had meant better schools for Tanya, safer neighborhoods ... more opportunities.

The few men in Shaniece's life had been carefully chosen, and thoroughly researched. There was David, the accountant who'd lasted eight months until his passive-aggressive comments about their "non-traditional family" had earned him a swift dismissal. Then Robert, the pharmaceutical sales rep who'd seemed perfect until he'd revealed his expectation that Shaniece would scale back her career after marriage.

Tanya zipped her toiletry bag with more force than necessary. Her mother had never needed a man. They'd built their life brick by careful brick, supporting each other through every milestone. When Tanya got her first gallery job, Shaniece had thrown her a celebration dinner in their new condo's dining room—a far cry from the fold-out card table of their early years.

The sound of tape tearing echoed in her bedroom as she secured her travel-sized bottles. That same methodical approach had governed everything in their lives, from college applications to investment strategies. Her mother wasn't the type to get swept up in some Parisian romance like a lovestruck teenager.

"A month," Tanya muttered, checking her passport's expiration date. "She wants to marry a stranger in a month." The passport photo stared back at her, showing the same determined expression she'd inherited from her mother—the look that had gotten them through endless late nights, tight budgets, and every obstacle life had thrown their way.

She pulled up Bernard François Dubois name on her phone, fingers flying across the screen as she dug through social media and news articles.

Dubois Properties.

Real estate empire.

Old French money.

The kind of wealth that could make someone disappear into a foreign country, leaving their entire life behind.

The thought seized her chest like a vise. They'd never needed anyone else. Through school plays and swim meets, college tours, and first heartbreaks, it had been the two of them against the world. Now some French businessman had swept in and threatened to dismantle everything they'd built.

Her carry-on clicked shut with finality. First the fourteen-hour flight, then she'd have time to make her mother see reason. To remind her of all the careful choices that had gotten them here. To protect her from making the kind of impulsive decision that could undo decades of calculated planning.

Tanya moved through her pre-travel checklist with practiced efficiency. Thermostat adjusted. Mail held. Security system armed. Each task a small piece of control in a situation that felt increasingly out of her hands.

Tanya lay in her king-sized bed, staring at the city lights playing across her ceiling. Her phone showed 3:47 AM. In less than two hours, she'd need to head to O'Hare for her flight, but sleep refused to come.

The blue glow from her tablet illuminated Bernard Dubois's corporate headshot. Silver-streaked dark hair, piercing green eyes, and a smile that probably charmed everything in a five-mile radius. Her research had revealed an impressive list of real estate holdings, charitable contributions, and society page appearances. No criminal record. No bankruptcies. No scandals.

She switched to images of his properties. Luxury high-rises in Paris, Monaco, and Geneva gleamed in professional photos. The kind of buildings where doormen wore white gloves and residents never asked about the price of anything.

Her mother deserved luxury. *But what if it came with strings? What if this man expected Shaniece to give up her career, her independence, her whole life in Chicago?*

Tanya rolled onto her side, punching her pillow into submission. The framed photo on her nightstand caught her eye – herself at age eight, gap-toothed and beaming, while her mother stood behind her with hands on her shoulders. They wore matching sundresses Shaniece had sewn herself, saving money for Tanya's summer camp tuition.

"We don't need handouts," her mother used to say. "We build our own dreams."

But Bernard Dubois wasn't offering handouts. He was offering a whole new life, complete with a centuries-old family name and property empire. The type of man who probably had staff to handle his staff.

Her mother's voice echoed in her memory: "When you know, you know."

But how could anyone know after just a few weeks? Love, at first sight, was for fairy tales and romantic comedies, not for brilliant marketing executives who'd built their success through careful strategy and measurable results.

Tanya grabbed her phone, pulling up her prepared talking points:

The list felt cold, clinical. Her mother wouldn't respond to bullet points and pie charts. This was the woman who'd taught her to trust her instincts, to recognize authentic art by the way it made her feel rather than its price tag.

But those instincts were screaming that something wasn't right.

The city's pre-dawn sounds filtered through her windows – early delivery trucks, distant L-train rumbles, the familiar rhythm of Chicago waking up. Soon she'd be in Paris, where everything would be different. Different language, different customs, different expectations of what a woman should be.

Her closet door stood open, the packed suitcase a silent sentinel. The black cocktail dress hung visible through the garment bag, ready for whatever formal occasions awaited in Paris. Would she be expected to play the dutiful almost-stepdaughter, smiling and nodding at dinner parties while her mother disappeared into this man's world?

"You're being dramatic," she muttered to her ceiling.

But the knot in her stomach wouldn't loosen. This wasn't about Bernard's wealth or status. It was about watching her mother – her brilliant, independent, calculated-risk-taking mother – transform into someone who made life-altering decisions based on feelings.

The bedside clock ticked to 4:15 AM. Tanya sat up, abandoning any pretense of sleep. Her reflection in the bathroom mirror showed dark circles under her eyes, but makeup would cover those. She'd learned that trick from her mother too – how to look polished and in control even when everything felt like it was spinning sideways.

She stepped into the shower, letting the hot water pound against her shoulders. The speech she'd rehearsed all night played through her mind:

"Mama, I support your happiness, but..."

"Have you considered the implications of..."

"What if we take some time to..."

Each opening line felt inadequate. *How do you tell the woman who taught you to chase your dreams that her dream might be a mistake? How do you protect someone who's spent their whole life protecting you?*

The water ran cold before she had an answer.

ord to cdg

Chicago O'Hare International Airport

Tanya settled into her first-class seat, the plush fabric enveloping her like a warm embrace. She adjusted her scarf, the slight chill of the cabin air pressing against her neck, and finally folded her hands over her lap. As the plane began its ascent, a small part of her felt guilty for enjoying this luxury, but she brushed it aside. *She had earned it.* Years spent curating art, networking, and navigating the politics of the gallery world had paid off, and the comfort of first class, complete with a glass of champagne waiting at her side, was a reflection of that hard work. Yet, deep down, the clink of the glass rang like a reminder—something was still missing.

Her gaze drifted to the clouds outside, white and fluffy, stretching endlessly against the blue sky. Tanya thought of her Mama, at that age—a single parent, working multiple jobs just to make ends meet. Back then, how different their realities had been. Shaniece juggled the grit of life, while Tanya now faced the privilege of choice. But with every triumph in her career, the void in her heart grew wider. *How could she be fiercely independent, own a gallery, and still feel unfulfilled?*

The seatbelt sign turned off, and she opened the sleek black notebook she always carried, its pages filled with musings and sketches. The recollection of her Mama's excited voice still echoed in her ears. Shaniece had sounded so alive. "I've met the love of my life, Tanya! His name is Bernard."

Bernard.

The name lingered uneasily in Tanya's mind. *Did love truly strike so suddenly? Hadn't her Mama taught her to be cautious?* No, Shaniece had taught her to believe. She stifled a sigh and leaned back in her seat, allowing her emotions to ebb and flow like the turbulence she knew she would face soon.

As the plane leveled off, Tanya's thoughts drifted to her own romantic history. A series of fleeting encounters and disappointing relationships mixed with anger and regret spun in her mind like an out-of-control carousel. Devon, with his charming smile and smooth words, had turned out to be a man with hidden commitments. She still recalled the sickening feeling splashed across her chest when evidence of his marital status became undeniable.

Then came Marcus, the artist, and a little shit. There had been something so intoxicating about his passion for paint and canvases, but his dreaminess had quickly turned into a nightmare of avoidance. He loved the idea of love, but not the reality it demanded. With him, she had experienced nights lost in flames of excitement, only for dawn to bring an empty silence.

James was different, or so she thought. An entrepreneur who promised spontaneity and adventure—yet every night curled in his embrace turned into a labyrinth of gambling stories that left her emotionally drained.

Turbulence jolted the plane, shaking Tanya from her reverie. She took a deep breath, feeling the reminder that her relationships were mere echoes of what she truly wanted. She recalled Michelle's wedding, bright and blooming with joy, her friend marrying a steady, thoughtful man. The kind of man Tanya secretly envied yet never allowed herself to want. She shoved her fingers through her locs and groaned softly. *Why did she keep choosing men who flaunted excitement like a trophy?*

The aircraft lurched again, and she gripped the armrests, her heart racing. There it was—her instinct for self-preservation. She had always chased the thrill, the adrenaline, but what had that brought her? She wondered if her propensity for the adventurous had masked her longing for something more authentic—someone real to look into the eye.

With the light of Paris rapidly approaching outside the window, she let her mind wander toward her Mama's description of Bernard. A real estate magnate, refined with charm. On paper, he seemed perfect, yet Tanya had always trusted her instincts, and they warned her that nothing like this ever happened without consequences. The city's lights glittered below, reminding her of Kendrick, the doctor who had faded like an unsent text message, the one whose timing had never aligned with hers. Their paths never intertwined in the way she had dreamed.

Tanya traced her finger along the rim of her champagne glass, the memory of Kendrick rising unbidden like smoke from dying embers. His chocolate skin, those deep-set eyes that crinkled when he smiled, and that brilliant mind that could diagnose complex medical cases within minutes. Every part of him had seemed sculpted by divine hands.

Their connection blazed from the moment they met at a charity gala. Between discussing African art and debating healthcare policies, sparks had caught fire. His passion for medicine matched her love of art—both healers in their own way, he'd said. Those words had melted her usual defenses.

The flight attendant stopped by, offering fresh drinks. Tanya declined with a slight shake of her head. She didn't need alcohol to remind her of those endless nights waiting for Kendrick to finish his shifts, of elaborate dinners gone cold, of museum dates canceled at the last minute. Each time, his apologies came wrapped in dedication to his patients, in stories of lives saved, in promises of "next time."

But next time never came.

Their relationship existed in the margins of his schedule—quick coffee dates between rounds, hurried kisses in hospital parking lots, text messages that went unanswered for hours. She'd convinced herself it was enough, that loving a doctor meant accepting this fractured kind of romance.

The truth had struck during a gallery opening, her biggest show to date. She'd reserved a front-row seat for him, right next to her Mama. The empty chair mocked her throughout her speech. His text arrived three hours later: **"Emergency surgery. Sorry. Make it up to you."**

The words blurred on her phone screen that night, tears falling as she finally admitted what she'd known for months. Kendrick loved her, yes—but he loved his calling more. She'd never compete with the rush of the ER, the satisfaction of saving lives, the absolute certainty of his purpose.

Her fingers clenched around the armrest as the plane hit another patch of turbulence. The physical jolt matched the emotional one in her chest. Even now, two years later, the pain lingered. Not because Kendrick had been cruel or unfaithful, but because their love had been real—just not enough. Not enough to bridge the gap between their worlds, not enough to make him choose her over his calling.

The passenger next to her shifted, reminding Tanya to loosen her grip on the armrest. She exhaled slowly, watching city lights twinkle below like scattered diamonds. Kendrick had taught her the hardest lesson: love alone wasn't enough. It needed nurturing, presence, commitment beyond words and intentions.

That's what worried her about her Mama's sudden engagement. *How well could Mama know this Bernard? How could she be sure his love would translate into presence, into partnership?* The Atlantic Ocean stretched between Chicago and Paris like a metaphor for all the potential obstacles.

Her Mama deserved more than beautiful words and empty promises. She deserved someone who would show up, who would make space in their life for love. Tanya had watched her Mama sacrifice everything to raise her, working endless hours, postponing her own dreams. Now that Tanya was successful, it was her turn to protect her Mama from potential heartbreak.

The irony wasn't lost on her. Here she sat, flying first class to Paris, while her thoughts circled around a man who had never made time to attend a single one of her gallery openings. Kendrick probably still worked those impossible hours, still saved lives, still left someone else waiting for his attention.

A part of her—the part that still believed in fairy tales despite everything—wondered if he ever thought about her. If he ever passed by her gallery and remembered their conversations about art and healing. If he ever regretted not trying harder to balance his two loves.

But that part of her needed to stay buried, especially now. She had a mission in Paris, and it didn't involve dwelling on past heartbreaks. Her Mama needed her clear-headed and focused, not lost in memories of a love that had slipped through her fingers like grains of sand.

"Why is love so complicated?" Tanya whispered, voicing the question into the cushion of her seat. The cabin remained silent, merely returning her thought, and yet the weight in her chest grew heavier.

The steady hum of jet engines mixed with the soft classical music playing through Tanya's noise-canceling headphones. Her eyelids grew heavy as exhaustion crept in, her body finally surrendering to the emotional toll of the past twenty-four hours. The leather seat cradled her like a cocoon as she drifted between consciousness and sleep.

Images floated through her mind: her mother's radiant face on FaceTime, the rushed gallery preparations, the hasty packing. They swirled together like watercolors bleeding into each other. Her last coherent thought focused on the black cocktail dress, still wrapped in tissue paper at the bottom of her carry-on.

Dreams came in fragments. She stood in an empty gallery, walls stretching endlessly in every direction. Each painting featured her mother's face—young, old, laughing, serious—captured in different moments of their shared life. The frames morphed from simple wood to ornate gold, then shifted into window frames looking out over Paris.

Her subconscious painted pictures of a faceless Bernard, his outline blurry and indistinct. In her dream, he transformed from a sophisticated businessman into a cartoon villain, complete with twirling mustache. The absurdity of it made her dream-self laugh, the sound echoing through empty gallery halls.

The scene changed. She was three years old again, watching her father walk out the door. Only this time, he wore a beret and spoke with a French accent. Her mother's voice called from somewhere distant, speaking words she couldn't quite grasp.

Time stretched like taffy in her dreams. One moment she was a child, clutching her mother's hand as they walked through the Art Institute of Chicago. The next, she stood alone in front of the Eiffel Tower, its iron framework disappearing into storm clouds above.

Her breathing deepened, body relaxing despite the turbulent images in her mind. The first-class cabin's climate control kept her at the perfect temperature, and someone – probably a flight attendant – had draped a soft blanket over her legs.

Fragments of conversations with her mother drifted through her dreams. "Love doesn't always make sense, baby." The words echoed in her mother's voice, from a long-ago discussion about her first heartbreak in high school. "Sometimes it just hits you like lightning."

The dream shifted again. She stood in front of a mirror, wearing her mother's wedding dress. But when she looked at her reflection, she saw her mother's face instead of her own. Their features blended together until she couldn't tell where one ended and the other began.

Her unconscious mind churned through fears and hopes, spinning them into surreal tableaux. A Paris street transformed into Lake Shore Drive. French pastries morphed into her mother's Sunday morning pancakes. Art pieces from her gallery danced with classical sculptures from the Louvre.

Through it all, a persistent thought threaded its way: What if her mother had found something real? What if true love could strike like lightning, leaving you forever changed? The questions followed her through dream after dream, never quite finding answers.

Hours passed as Tanya slept, her body adjusting to the changing time zones even as her mind processed her fears through dreams.

The plane crossed ocean and continent, carrying her closer to Paris with each passing minute. Closer to answers she wasn't sure she wanted to find.

Her dreaming mind painted pictures of possible futures: holiday dinners with French relatives, her mother living in a foreign country, FaceTime calls replacing their Sunday brunches. Each scenario brought fresh waves of anxiety, even in sleep. Her fingers twitched beneath the blanket, reaching for something – or someone – just out of reach.

The cabin lights dimmed and brightened with the passing hours, but Tanya remained lost in her dreams. Flight attendants moved quietly past her seat, their soft footsteps and whispered conversations becoming part of her dreamscape. In her mind, their voices transformed into art gallery patrons discussing her mother's love life in hushed, critical tones.

Tanya woke up to the flight crew announcing their descent into Charles de Gaulle Airport, and she straightened and prepared herself for the hustle below. Exhaustion pulled at her limbs. She watched as the rumble of wheels engulfed her heart, a bittersweet sensation mixing hope with skepticism.

Stepping off the plane, generations of anticipation guided her to baggage claim. The airport buzzed with excitement, couples embracing, families reuniting, but Tanya felt like an observer on the sidelines. She maneuvered through the throng of passengers, her suitcase rolling silently beside her like an unsent postcard. She retrieved her bags with practiced efficiency and snatched a breath after the long flight, reminding herself she had a responsibility—her Mama's happiness depended on her.

Tanya stepped outside to a cool evening breeze, soaking in the lively atmosphere of Paris. A car service awaited her with a polite driver holding a sign embossed with her name. As she climbed into the back seat, the nerve-wracking pursuit of her Mama's whirlwind romance loomed ahead. She needed to gather her thoughts before facing the reality of her Mama's choices—choices that would ripple through their lives forever.

During the ride, shades of twilight wrapped Paris in a shimmer, but Tanya barely glanced out the window. Instead, her mind raced. She didn't want to be that person—the one who questioned her Mama's decisions. But what if this romance was a bad idea after all?

"I need a drink," she murmured to herself.

an evening in montmartre
. . .

The metro steps deposited Tanya into a Montmartre evening that felt pulled from a romance movie. Golden light spilled across cobblestones as a saxophonist's melodies drifted through the warm air. Couples wound their way through the narrow streets, lost in private worlds of whispered jokes and stolen kisses.

Her heels clicked against ancient stones as she wandered past crowded cafes, their tables spilling onto sidewalks in a chaos of glasses clinking and animated French conversation. The sheer density of happiness around her made her solitude feel more acute.

A small wine bar caught her eye—all exposed brick and copper accents gleaming under Edison bulbs. Through the window, she spotted a single empty seat at the bar. *Perfect.*

The space enveloped her in warmth and the rich scent of red wine. Vintage jazz played at just the right volume to allow intimate conversation while maintaining privacy. Couples occupied every table, heads bent close together over shared bottles and small plates.

"Bonsoir." She slid onto the last leather barstool, pleased when the bartender responded in English after hearing her accent. "I'll have whatever Bordeaux you recommend."

The antique mirror behind the bar reflected the room in soft focus, letting her people watch discretely while sipping her wine.

Through the mirror's reflection, Tanya watched the steady flow of people pairing up around her. A guy in a navy blazer leaned in close to whisper something to his date, making her throw her head back in genuine laughter. Another couple fed each other bites of cheese, trading soft kisses between sips of wine.

Her own reflection stared back at her - hair still perfectly styled despite the humidity, makeup intact after the long flight. She looked exactly like what she was: a woman who'd crossed an ocean to stop her mother from making an impulsive mistake. The irony wasn't lost on her.

At a corner table, three French women commanded attention with their easy confidence. Designer bags hung casually from their chairs while they gestured with lit cigarettes, their laughter floating above the general buzz of conversation. One woman with a sleek bob caught Tanya's eye in the mirror and raised her glass in a small salute of solidarity.

Tanya lifted her own glass in return, admiring how they embodied that effortless Parisian style she'd always envied. No perfectly coordinated outfits or careful makeup—just well-cut basics and that indefinable French attitude that made everything look intentional.

Her wine arrived—a rich Bordeaux that tasted of blackberries and oak. The first sip helped unknot some of the tension she'd been carrying since her mother's call. The second sip had her wondering if maybe she'd overreacted. Her Mama wasn't some lovesick teenager. She was a grown woman who'd successfully raised a daughter alone while building a career.

A flash of movement caught her attention—a tall figure in a perfectly tailored navy suit declining someone's advances with practiced grace.

Her breath caught as she studied him in the mirror. Strong jaw, wavy dark hair, and striking blue eyes that somehow managed to convey both warmth and intensity. He moved with the easy confidence of someone completely comfortable in their own skin.

When he turned, their eyes met in the mirror. A slight smile played at the corners of his mouth as he made his way to the empty space beside her. His cologne reached her first—subtle notes of cedar and bergamot that made her want to lean closer.

"This seat taken?"

The voice came from behind her left shoulder—deep, masculine, colored with a French accent that somehow made those three simple words sound like poetry. Tanya kept her eyes on the mirror, using it to observe the man who'd materialized beside her barstool.

Tall. Broad-shouldered but lean, like a swimmer. He wore a white button-down with the sleeves rolled to expose strong forearms, and dark jeans that fit exactly right.

The kind of man she normally avoided because they spelled trouble with a capital T.

The kind of man who, on any other night, she would have dismissed with a polite but firm "sorry, not interested."

But something about being in Paris, about watching all these couples lost in their private moments of joy, about her mother throwing caution to the wind and choosing love... it made her turn slightly on her stool and gesture to the empty seat beside her.

"It is now."

The corner of his mouth lifted in a smile that transformed his whole face from merely handsome to devastating. He slid onto the stool with easy grace, and that's when she caught his full scent—something woodsy and expensive that made her want to touch him.

"You're stunning," he said, extending his hand.

His palm was warm against hers, the handshake lingering a beat longer than strictly necessary. "So are you."

"American?" His accent wrapped around the word like silk.

"That obvious?"

"The accent gives you away. But also..." He gestured to her empty wine glass. "You drink like you mean business. French women, they make one glass last all evening."

"Are you criticizing my drinking habits?" She signaled the bartender for another round.

"Not at all. I admire a woman who knows what she wants." His eyes met hers in the mirror, and the heat in his gaze made her pulse skip.

The bartender placed fresh glasses in front of them both, and he raised his in a toast. "To happy accidents."

"Is that what this is?" She clinked her glass against his, holding his gaze.

"You tell me. Beautiful woman, sitting alone in a wine bar in the most romantic neighborhood in Paris? Either you're waiting for someone, or…"

"Or?"

"Or you're open to possibilities."

ALEXANDRE HAD WATCHED her from the moment she entered. The way she moved through the crowded bar with quiet confidence caught his attention immediately. Her casual attire and natural hair styled in locs spoke of someone comfortable in her own skin.

He'd spent the evening deflecting advances from the usual crowd that frequented this bar—trust fund girls and tourists looking for their French romance fantasy. But this woman was different. She carried herself with a sophistication that made the other women fade into background noise.

The sight of her stirred memories of Adrienne. His ex had possessed that same self-assured grace, the kind that came from knowing exactly who you were. But where Adrienne had been all sharp edges and ambition, this woman had a softness around her eyes that hinted at depth beneath her polished exterior.

"Another Scotch, monsieur?" The bartender's question pulled him from his thoughts.

Alexandre waved him off, his attention drawn back to the woman's reflection in the mirror. She was people-watching, but not with the obvious eagerness of a tourist. Her gaze was analytical, almost academic in its detachment. The way she held her wine glass - stem between two fingers, swirling gently—suggested someone who appreciated quality without showing off.

His phone buzzed. Another email from the Singapore office about the development project. Last year, messages like these would have sent him rushing back to his laptop, regardless of the hour. That workaholism had ultimately driven Adrienne away. "You're married to your work," she'd said during their final argument. "I'm tired of competing with spreadsheets for your attention."

She hadn't been wrong. The night she'd left, he'd barely looked up from his computer as she'd packed her bags. By the time he'd realized what he'd lost, she'd already moved back to Tortola.

The woman at the bar took another sip of wine, and the movement caught the light, highlighting her high cheekbones and full lips. Something about her stillness amid the bar's chaos drew him in. While others chatted and laughed too loudly, she observed with a quiet intensity that matched his own tendency toward careful assessment.

When their eyes met in the mirror, the connection was immediate and electric. Her gaze held his for a long moment before she looked away, but not before he caught the flash of interest in her expression.

He adjusted his cuffs—a nervous habit he thought he'd outgrown—and stood. This wasn't his usual approach. Typically, women came to him, drawn by his name or reputation. The few times he'd pursued someone, it had been with careful strategy, like preparing for a business negotiation.

But something about this woman made him want to abandon his usual calculated restraint. Perhaps it was the way she sat slightly apart from the crowd while remaining completely at ease. Or maybe it was simply that she reminded him of what he'd been missing since Adrienne—the challenge of engaging with someone who wouldn't be impressed by his surname or bank account.

As he approached, he caught the subtle scent of her perfume—something warm and spicy that made him think of summer nights. Up close, her skin glowed like honey under the bar's soft lighting. When she turned slightly at his approach, he noticed she wore no ring.

The space beside her felt charged with possibility. Alexandre realized he was more nervous than he'd been in years. This wasn't about finding a brief distraction or adding another conquest to his list. The pull he felt toward her was something altogether different - more primal and yet somehow more meaningful.

He gathered his courage and spoke. "This seat taken?"

Her response, when it came, carried a hint of amusement that suggested she'd been aware of his internal debate. "It is now."

The simple phrase held volumes—acknowledgment of mutual attraction, permission to proceed, but also a subtle challenge. She wasn't going to make this easy for him. The realization sent a thrill through him that had nothing to do with physical attraction and everything to do with the prospect of engaging with someone who might actually understand him.

TIME SLIPPED AWAY as they talked, their conversation flowing as smoothly as the wine. Tanya found herself leaning closer, drawn in by his mix of sharp intelligence and playful charm. He spoke about architecture and art with genuine passion, his eyes lighting up when she mentioned her work in contemporary galleries.

"So you have an eye for beauty." His fingers brushed against hers as he reached for his glass.

"Among other things." The wine had loosened her usual reserve, making her bold. "I appreciate quality in all its forms."

His gaze traveled over her face, lingering on her lips. "And what qualities do you look for?"

"Authenticity. Depth." She met his eyes. "Surprise."

"And have I surprised you?"

"By not being exactly what I expected? Yes."

He shifted closer, his knee brushing against hers. "What did you expect?"

"The usual. Some wealthy playboy looking for a tourist to seduce." She traced the rim of her glass. "But you're different."

"Different how?"

"You actually listen when I speak. Most men like you—" She caught herself. "Most men who look like you are too busy planning their next move to hear anything beyond yes or no."

His laugh was low and rich. "Men who look like me?"

"You know exactly how attractive you are." She gave him a knowing look. "False modesty doesn't suit you."

"Neither does it suit you." His hand found her knee under the bar, the touch sending electricity through her. "You're well aware of the effect you have."

The bar had grown more crowded, forcing them to lean in close to hear each other. His cologne mixed with the wine's bouquet, creating an intoxicating combination that made her head spin.

"Tell me," he said, voice dropping lower, "what brings you to Paris? Business or pleasure?"

"Neither. Or both." She smiled. "Let's say I'm open to possibilities."

"Possibilities." His thumb traced small circles on her knee. "Like what?"

"Like..." She took another sip of wine, letting the rich flavor roll over her tongue. "Like not overthinking everything for once."

"Overthinking can be overrated." His eyes held hers. "Sometimes the body knows what it wants before the mind catches up."

Heat bloomed in her chest, spreading outward. The noise of the bar faded to a distant hum as awareness centered on the points of contact between them—his knee against hers, his hand on her leg, the way their shoulders brushed when either of them moved.

"We should find somewhere quieter," he suggested, voice rough. "To continue our conversation."

The responsible part of her brain—the part that always calculated risks and consequences—tried to raise objections. But the wine, the Paris evening, and the magnetic pull between them had awakened something wild and reckless in her blood.

She leaned in close, letting her lips brush his ear. "My hotel is three blocks away."

His sharp intake of breath sent satisfaction coursing through her. When he pulled back to look at her, the raw desire in his expression made her pulse race.

"Are you sure?"

The question held genuine concern beneath the hunger. Another surprise from a man who kept defying her expectations.

"Yes." She stood, enjoying how his eyes followed the movement. "Unless you're overthinking things now?"

He laughed, the sound sending shivers down her spine. "Not at all." His hand settled at the small of her back as they made their way to the bar to settle their tab.

Outside, the Montmartre evening had transformed. The streets felt charged with possibility, the warm air heavy with promise. They walked close together, not quite touching but hyperaware of each other's presence.

"Your hotel?" he asked when they reached an intersection.

She pointed left. "The Terrass."

"Ah, excellent choice. The rooftop bar has the best view of the city."

"I wouldn't know. I haven't seen it yet."

His smile held wicked promise. "Perhaps we can remedy that later."

They reached the hotel entrance, its art deco facade glowing softly in the evening light. Tanya paused, giving him one last chance to back out. "Coming up?"

He caught her hand, bringing it to his lips. The kiss he pressed to her palm was surprisingly tender. "Lead the way."

the morning after
. . .

*P*ale light filtered through gauzy curtains as Alexandre's eyes fluttered open. His mind pieced together unfamiliar elements - cream-colored walls, generic artwork, the faint hum of an air conditioner. Not his Left Bank apartment. A hotel room.

His muscles ached in the most pleasant way as fragments of the night before crystallized in his consciousness. The wine bar in Montmartre. Walking past it after a grueling day of meetings, intending only to have one glass before heading home. Then seeing her.

He turned his head on the pillow, careful not to disturb the mattress. She lay on her stomach, the white sheet draped low across her hips. Her bare back caught the dim light, smooth dark skin seeming to glow. Wild curls spilled across the pillow, a few strands falling across her face. Her lips, still slightly swollen from his kisses, were parted in sleep.

What was her name? He furrowed his brow, trying to recall if they'd even exchanged that basic detail. Their conversation at the bar had flowed effortlessly from art to travel to wine, punctuated by loaded glances and "accidental" touches. But names? He'd been too captivated by her quick wit and the way her eyes crinkled when she laughed.

The memory of her at the bar surfaced - perched on that stool in casual attire dressed in natural beauty. The way she'd deflected that drunken American tourist with such grace, then caught Alexandre's appreciative smile in the mirror. Her slight accent - American, but with rounded vowels that hinted at private schools and cultural refinement.

He remembered how she'd tasted of the Bordeaux they'd shared, when he'd finally kissed her in the taxi. How she'd pulled him closer by his tie, whispering directions to her hotel between heated breaths. The elevator ride felt endless, her back pressed against the mirrored wall as his hands mapped the curves of her waist.

Now, in the gathering dawn, Alexandre found himself wanting more than just the memory of one passionate night. He wanted her name, her story, her phone number. Wanted to take her to his favorite hidden bistro in Le Marais, to show her the secret gardens he'd discovered on his morning runs through the city.

But something in the way she'd kissed him—fierce yet somehow distant—suggested she'd wanted only this: one perfect night with a stranger in Paris—a Paris fling. The thought left an unexpected hollow feeling in his chest.

A siren wailed in the distance, and she stirred slightly. Her shoulder blade shifted under silk-smooth skin as she nestled deeper into the pillow. The sheet slipped lower, revealing the subtle dimples at the base of her spine. His fingers itched to trace them, to wake her with soft kisses along her shoulder blades. To suggest breakfast at the cafe he could see through the window, where they could linger over coffee and croissants while learning each other's names.

Instead, he lay still, watching the play of early light across her skin. Their joining had been passionate but tender—hands exploring, breath mingling, bodies moving in perfect rhythm. He'd discovered a small tattoo on her hip, an infinity symbol wrapped around a compass rose. When he'd traced it with his tongue, she'd gasped the word '*fuck*' in a way that still echoed in his mind.

She'd been full of delicious contradictions. The sophisticated woman who'd matched his knowledge of Renaissance masters, yet danced with abandoned grace when he'd turned on the room's bluetooth speaker. The woman who'd taken charge in the elevator but yielded so sweetly in bed. Her controlled exterior had melted away beneath his touch, revealing something wild and free.

Alexandre shifted slightly, his body responding to the memories. The motion made his watch catch the light, and he glimpsed the time. Six AM. He had a breakfast meeting at eight with potential investors—a meeting he should already be preparing for. Yet he found himself reluctant to leave this bubble of anonymous intimacy.

Alexandre eased himself from beneath the tangled sheets, his movements careful not to disturb the sleeping beauty beside him.

He gathered his scattered clothing—a designer shirt from the lampshade, pants from beside the chaise lounge, a tie from the nightstand. Each item a breadcrumb trail of their passionate night. His fingers brushed the spot where she'd gripped his tie, using it to pull him close for that first searing kiss.

The urge to wake her, to ask her name, to suggest breakfast struck him with unexpected force. But that wasn't what this was about. They'd both known it when they'd left the wine bar together, the understanding clear in every heated glance and deliberate touch.

He dressed in the bathroom, splashing cold water on his face and finger-combing his disheveled hair. His reflection showed stubble and tired eyes, but his lips curved in satisfaction. The memory of her taste, her sighs, the way she'd matched his passion with her own would stay with him.

At the door, Alexandre paused for one final look. She'd shifted in her sleep, one arm reaching across the space he'd vacated. The sheet had slipped lower, revealing the smooth expanse of her back. He forced himself to turn away, easing the door shut with a soft click.

TANYA'S EYES snapped open at the sound. For a moment, she lay still, processing the empty space beside her and the lingering warmth on the sheets. Her mystery Frenchman had done exactly what she'd expected—what she'd wanted him to do.

"Perfect," she murmured, stretching luxuriously. Her body held pleasant reminders of their night together—the good kind of ache that came from hours of passionate sex. No awkward morning-after conversation, no fumbling exchange of numbers they'd never use. Just a beautiful memory to take home with her.

She padded to the bathroom, catching glimpses of herself in the gilt-edged mirrors that seemed to multiply her reflection into infinity. A satisfied smile played across her lips as she turned the water on to fill the tub, adding a generous splash of the hotel's fancy lavender bath oil. Turning around towards the mirror again, her eyes lowered towards her breasts, still tender from his passionate attention. Her perfect porn star C's—*shit,* she'd spent enough on them to fund a small car—but moments like these made every penny worth it. She silently thanked God her mystery

Frenchman had been exactly the type to appreciate quality craftsmanship, his skilled hands making her forget they weren't entirely natural.

Hot water sluiced over her skin as steam filled the marble enclosure. Tanya swished her bare limbs around in the hot water, her eyes closed as she relived the passionate night before. She wasn't that drunk to remember his hot kisses down her neck, the way he undressed her, the way he entered her over and over throughout the night. The memory of his body pressed against hers, his breath hot against her skin, sent shivers down her spine.

As she lay back in the tub, she couldn't help but wonder about him. *Who was this mysterious Frenchman? What was his name? Where did he come from?* But then she reminded herself that this was exactly what she wanted—a one-night stand with no strings attached. She didn't need to know anything about him beyond what they had shared in bed.

Her thoughts drifted back to their encounter. It had been intense, almost animalistic at times. But there had also been a tenderness between them that surprised her. He had looked into her eyes as if seeing something deep within her soul, and it had made her feel exposed yet vulnerable at the same time.

While Tanya bathed in the tub, she found herself running her fingers over the places where he had caressed her before. The mere thought of his hands on her flesh elicited a rush of pleasure that coursed through her body. A soft moan escaped her lips as she envisioned him repeating the act, his lips tracing a path of kisses down her neck, his fingers discovering every curve and crevice of her body. She felt a shiver run down her spine as she remembered the way his fingers had teased her nipples, eliciting gasps of pleasure. The sensation of his tongue on her skin was still fresh in her mind, and she could feel herself growing wet at the memory. She let out a sigh as she slid her fingers lower, tracing the outline of her hip before moving to the apex of her thighs. She could still feel the weight of his body on top of hers, the way he had thrust into her with an urgency that left her breathless. She closed her eyes and let herself get lost in the memory, her body responding to the mental images with a growing need for release.

Tanya reached for the soap, its slickness reminding her of his tongue gliding over her skin. She trailed the bar over her stomach, feeling the suds pool in her belly button before continuing lower. Her fingers grazed the soft hair between her legs before delving into the slick folds. She could almost feel his lips on her clit as she circled it with her fingers, imagining the way he had lapped at her with a fervor that left her panting. The memory of his tongue darting inside her sent a shiver down her spine, and she pressed her fingers deeper, mimicking the rhythm of his thrusts. She bit her lip as the pressure built, her body writhing under the onslaught of sensations.

As Tanya's fingers plunged deeper, her other hand abandoned the side of the tub to find her breast. She recalled the way he had teased her nipples, grazing them with his teeth before flicking his tongue over the sensitive peaks. The memory was enough to send her over the edge, and she pinched her nipple between her fingers, imagining the sting of his teeth. Her body shook as the orgasm washed over her, her muscles contracting around her fingers. She let out a low moan, the sound echoing in the small bathroom as she rode out the waves of pleasure.

Tanya let go a sigh and laid her head back on the rim of the tub. Their encounter had been exactly what she needed —wild, uninhibited, and safely contained within the fantasy of a Parisian night.

Tanya got out of the tub and wrapped herself in the hotel's plush robe, walking back into the bed area, she checked her phone.

Seven texts from her mother, each more excited than the last, arranging their meeting. She typed a quick response, suggesting a cafe near her hotel.

"Just got your messages. Bath and coffee, then I'm all yours. Send me the address?"

Her mother's reply came instantly, complete with multiple heart emojis. Tanya shook her head, amused by Shaniece's uncharacteristic giddiness. She pulled out a sleek white pantsuit - professional enough to meet her mother's fiancé, but with enough edge to remind everyone she wasn't here to play happy families.

The events of last night could stay locked away with her other memories of beautiful strangers in foreign cities. Right now, she needed to focus on why she'd really come to Paris—making sure her mother wasn't making the biggest mistake of her life.

She gave her reflection a final check, adjusting her locs and touching up her lipstick. The woman in the mirror looked composed, controlled, ready to face whatever came next. No one would guess she'd spent the night moaning in pleasure under the skilled hands of a nameless Frenchman.

Tanya grabbed her phone and designer tote, heading for the door. Her mother's next text showed a cafe just two blocks away. Time to switch gears from passionate stranger to protective daughter.

parisian café

. . .

Golden morning light spilled across the checkered tablecloth as Tanya watched her mother practically float toward their café table. Shaniece's coral silk dress caught the breeze, her radiant smile visible from half a block away. The sight squeezed Tanya's heart - she hadn't seen her mother this carefree since... well, ever.

"Baby girl!" Shaniece wrapped Tanya in a tight embrace, her familiar jasmine perfume mixing with fresh-baked croissants from the café. "I can't believe you're actually here. You look tired though - jet lag?"

Tanya adjusted her oversized sunglasses, grateful they hid the shadows under her eyes. "Something like that." She sank into the wrought-iron chair, pushing aside memories of tangled sheets and whispered French endearments.

"You have to hear how I met Bernard." Shaniece's fingers wrapped around her café au lait. "I was at Le Meurice for that cosmetics conference, completely lost trying to find the meeting room. This distinguished gentleman offered to help, and the moment our eyes met..." She pressed a hand to her chest. "It sounds crazy, but I just knew."

"Knew what exactly?" Tanya stirred her espresso, the spoon clinking against fine china.

"That he was the one. We spent the entire afternoon walking through the Tuileries Garden. He showed me his favorite hidden spots in the city, told me stories about growing up here." Shaniece's eyes sparkled. "By dinner, it felt like I'd known him my whole life."

"Mama, that's..." Tanya paused, choosing her words carefully. "That's a beautiful story. But don't you think this is moving incredibly fast? You've only known him for what - three weeks?"

"When you know, you know." Shaniece reached across the table, covering Tanya's hand with her own. "Bernard understands me in ways I can't even explain. The way he listens, *really* listens. How he remembers every little detail I mention. Did you know he had the hotel kitchen make my grandmother's sweet potato pie recipe for our second date?"

"That's thoughtful, but—"

"And he's so passionate about his work, just like me. We can talk for hours about everything and nothing," Shaniece's free hand gestured expressively. "He challenges me intellectually while making me feel completely safe to be vulnerable ... and the sex! Oh, my lord, *girl*—he's the best lover I ever had."

Tanya withdrew her hand, wrapping both palms around her coffee cup. "Mama ... I just worry about you getting hurt. People aren't always what they seem."

"You think I don't know that?" Shaniece's voice softened. "After everything with your father, trust me—I've got my eyes wide open. Bernard isn't some fantasy. He's *real*, flaws and all, and that's what makes this so special."

The mention of her father made Tanya's chest tighten. Her own reckless night burned in her throat, begging to be confessed. The irony of her judging her mother's whirlwind romance while the evidence of her own lingered on her skin wasn't lost on her.

"I hear you saying you're being careful," Tanya said. "But marriage? Already?"

"When you're our age, you stop wasting time playing games," Shaniece's fingers traced the rim of her cup. "We know who we are, what we want. Why wait when everything feels so right?"

Tanya opened her mouth, then closed it. The weight of her secret pressed against her chest. One perfect night with a stranger had left her feeling more alive than she had in years. Who was she to question her mother's happiness when she'd just thrown caution to the wind herself?

But no - this wasn't about her. This was about protecting her mother from potential heartbreak. Tanya swallowed the confession along with the last bitter sip of espresso.

"Tell me more about Bernard," she said instead. "I want to understand what makes him so special to you."

Shaniece's eyes lit up as she leaned forward. "Bernard runs Dubois Properties - they're one of the largest real estate developers in France. But he's not just about business. He supports local artists, sits on museum boards. Last week, he took me to this tiny gallery in Le Marais showcasing emerging African artists."

"A philanthropist real estate mogul?" Tanya arched an eyebrow. "Sounds almost too perfect."

"Oh, he has his quirks," Shaniece laughed. "He's absolutely particular about his coffee - won't touch anything but this specific Brazilian roast. And don't get me started on his sock organization system."

A waiter appeared with fresh pastries, giving Tanya a moment to gather her thoughts. "Has he been married before?"

"No, never married," Shaniece broke off a piece of croissant. "He was engaged once, years ago, but it didn't work out. He has a son from that relationship—he's about your age, actually."

Tanya's coffee cup clattered against its saucer. "A son? That's... unexpected."

"Bernard raised him as a single father. They're very close." Shaniece dabbed her lips with a napkin. "Which reminds me - we need to discuss the living arrangements."

"Living arrangements?"

"We've worked out a compromise for the first six months. One month here in Paris, one month in Chicago. That way we can both maintain our careers while we figure out a permanent solution."

The morning sun suddenly felt too bright against Tanya's face. "You're going to live in two different countries? Mama, that's not a marriage—that's extended dating with paperwork."

"It's temporary," Shaniece's voice took on the firm tone Tanya remembered from childhood arguments. "We're both established in our careers. Making a permanent move takes time and planning."

"And what happens after six months? One of you gives up everything you've built?"

"We'll cross that bridge when we come to it. The point is, we're willing to make compromises to be together."

"Compromise is one thing, but this sounds like chaos." Tanya pushed her plate away. "What about your job? Your friends? Our Sunday brunches?"

"Baby, you act like I'm disappearing forever," Shaniece reached across the table again. "We'll still have our brunches - they might just be in Paris sometimes. Think of it as an adventure."

"Adventures are for vacation, not marriage."

"Marriage is whatever two people decide it should be," Shaniece's chin lifted slightly. "Bernard and I connect on a level I've never experienced before. When we're together, everything just... flows. We understand each other without words. He anticipates what I need before I even know I need it."

"That's the honeymoon phase talking."

"No, it's different," Shaniece's voice softened. "Remember how I always told you that true love feels like coming home? That's what this is. When I'm with Bernard, I feel completely myself - no pretenses, no masks. Just me."

Tanya's protest died on her lips as she studied her mother's face. The joy radiating from Shaniece was undeniable, transforming her usual polished exterior into something luminous.

"We support each other's dreams," Shaniece continued. "He's as invested in my career as his own. Last week, he rearranged a board meeting just to attend my presentation to the European marketing team."

"And you really think this bi-continental arrangement will work?"

"I think love is worth trying for," Shaniece's fingers traced patterns on the tablecloth. "We're not naive teenagers. We've both built successful lives—raised children. Now we want to build something together, even if the path isn't traditional."

Tanya traced the rim of her empty espresso cup, her mother's words about love and connection stirring uncomfortable parallels in her mind. Her own reckless night hung between them, unspoken. The memory of her Frenchman's fingers trailing down her spine, his lips on her breasts, threatened to color her cheeks.

"What's going on in that head of yours?" Shaniece leaned forward, her maternal radar clearly picking up Tanya's distraction.

The words bubbled up in Tanya's throat. How easy it would be to tell her mother everything - the wine bar, the magnetic pull of attraction, the way she'd thrown her carefully constructed rules out the window for one perfect night. Her mother, of all people, might understand the allure of spontaneous passion in the City of Light.

But the timing felt wrong. Shaniece glowed with newfound happiness, her entire being radiating joy as she described her whirlwind romance. Tanya's anonymous encounter would only muddy the waters, raising questions about her judgment when she was trying to be the voice of reason.

"Just processing," Tanya adjusted her sunglasses. "It's a lot to take in."

"I know it seems crazy," Shaniece's fingers drummed against the table. "But sometimes the craziest choices lead us exactly where we need to be."

The irony of that statement wasn't lost on Tanya. Her own crazy choice had led her straight into a stranger's arms, leaving her with nothing but delicious memories and a slight hangover. But while her mother was building something real, Tanya had deliberately kept her encounter in the realm of fantasy - no names, no personal details, no future complications.

Through the cafe window, couples strolled past holding hands, their casual intimacy a stark reminder of what Tanya had always kept at arm's length. Her night with her mystery man had shown her a glimpse of what it felt like to let go completely, to trust in the moment without analyzing every possible outcome.

"Tell me more about the wedding plans," Tanya said instead, pushing her secret deeper. This moment belonged to her mother's happiness, not her own complicated feelings about love and connection.

"Are you sure?" Shaniece studied her face. "You seem… different today."

"Just jet lag," Tanya forced a smile. "And maybe a little culture shock. Paris is more overwhelming than I expected."

The lie felt small compared to the bigger truth she was withholding. As her mother launched into details about flower arrangements and venue options, Tanya's mind drifted to the way her Frenchman had looked at her in the bar mirror, as if he could see straight through her carefully maintained facade.

But that was precisely why such encounters needed to stay in their perfect bubble of anonymity. Real life was messy enough without adding international complications. Her mother's situation proved that point perfectly - juggling two continents, two careers, two entirely different lives.

No, Tanya decided firmly. Her Parisian interlude would remain exactly what it was meant to be - a beautiful memory, sealed away in the vault of things better left unsaid. She reached across the table and squeezed her mother's hand, channeling her energy into being present for this moment instead.

"So this wedding," Tanya straightened her shoulders. "When exactly are you thinking?"

the dubois residence
. . .

Tanya's fingers drummed against her thigh as the taxi wound through the elegant streets of the 16th arrondissement. Each mansion they passed seemed grander than the last, their limestone facades glowing golden in the late afternoon sun. Her mother had mentioned Bernard was successful, but this level of wealth hit differently.

The car slowed to a stop before massive wrought iron gates. Through the intricate metalwork, Tanya glimpsed a courtyard garden where perfectly manicured topiaries stood sentinel along a cobblestone drive. Her breath caught as the gates swung open with silent precision.

"This can't be right," Tanya double-checked the address on her phone, but the numbers matched.

The taxi crunched over the cobblestones, circling a burbling fountain where water trickled from the lips of bronze cherubs. The mansion loomed before them - three stories of Belle Époque splendor with tall windows and ornate balconies. Delicate iron railings traced geometric patterns across each terrace, and climbing roses framed the grand entrance.

Her palms grew damp. This wasn't just money - this was *old money*, generations of it carved into every architectural detail. The kind of wealth that made her gallery's most expensive pieces look like garage sale finds.

The driver pulled to a stop, and Tanya forced herself to breathe. She'd navigated plenty of high-stakes situations in her career. This was just another wealthy family, even if they were about to become *her* family too.

Thank God she wore her black cocktail dress, as she stepped out onto the cobblestones, her heels clicking against the stone. The sound echoed off the mansion's facade, making her feel small and exposed. Up close, she could see the patina of age on the limestone, the way decades of rain had softened its edges. This wasn't some nouveau riche McMansion - this was living history.

Movement caught her eye, and she spotted her mother emerging from the massive double doors. Shaniece practically floated down the steps, wrapped in a flowing silk dress that made her look like she'd already been living here for years.

"Baby girl!" Shaniece's face lit up. "Welcome to your new second home!"

Tanya managed a smile, but her eyes kept drifting up the mansion's facade. Through one of the upper windows, she glimpsed what looked like original artwork - the kind she'd only seen in museums. The kind her gallery would never be able to afford.

"Mama, when you said Bernard was comfortable..." Tanya gestured at their surroundings, letting the understatement hang in the air.

"I know, I know," Shaniece linked their arms together. "It's a lot to take in. But Bernard's not like that - he's the most down-to-earth man I've ever met. The family money doesn't define him."

Family money…

The words echoed in Tanya's head as she let her mother guide her toward the entrance. The doors stood at least twelve feet tall, their aged wood gleaming with countless layers of polish. Brass hardware glinted in the sunlight, and she noticed the door knocker bore an intricate family crest.

"The Dubois family has lived here for five generations," Shaniece explained, reading her daughter's expression. "But don't let it intimidate you. They're just people, same as us."

Just people who probably had more artwork in their foyer than her entire gallery. Tanya's steps faltered as they crossed the threshold into a soaring entry hall. A crystal chandelier cast rainbow prisms across marble floors, and a sweeping staircase curved up to the second floor. The walls showcased museum-worthy paintings, their gilt frames catching the light.

The scent of fresh flowers mixed with beeswax polish and something older - the subtle perfume of centuries of wealth and privilege. It filled her lungs with each breath, making her hyperaware of her outsider status.

Her mother squeezed her arm. "I know that look. Stop analyzing everything and just be open to getting to know them. Bernard's waited all day to meet you."

Tanya nodded, but her curator's eye couldn't help cataloging every detail. The antique Aubusson carpet beneath their feet. The Louis XV console table against one wall. The subtle security cameras disguised as architectural details. Each element spoke of carefully preserved privilege passed down through generations.

A door opened somewhere above them, and footsteps echoed from the second floor. Tanya straightened her spine and lifted her chin. Whatever happened next, she'd face it with the same poise she brought to her gallery openings. Even if every inch of this place reminded her just how far she was from her comfort zone.

Bernard descended the sweeping staircase with the fluid grace of someone born to navigate grand spaces. His silver-streaked dark hair and tailored clothes projected sophisticated ease, but it was his warm smile that caught Tanya off guard. She'd expected cold aristocratic refinement. Instead, his green eyes crinkled with genuine warmth as he approached, his focus entirely on her mother. The way Shaniece's whole being lit up at his presence spoke volumes.

"My darling," Bernard's rich baritone carried a hint of accent as he kissed Shaniece's cheek. He turned to Tanya, extending both hands in welcome. "And you must be Tanya. Your mother has told me so much about you - about your gallery, your eye for emerging artists. I'd love to show you some pieces from our family collection that might interest you professionally." His genuine interest in her work surprised her. Most collectors she dealt with treated her more like a sales clerk than a curator. But Bernard's questions about her latest exhibition revealed actual knowledge of the art world. Despite her lingering skepticism, Tanya found herself drawn into an animated discussion about an up-and-coming sculptor she'd recently discovered. The way Bernard listened intently, offering thoughtful insights without trying to dominate the conversation, hinted at why her practical mother had fallen so hard, so fast.

Tanya's heels clicked against the centuries-old wood as she followed her mother and Bernard through the grand entrance. Her eyes darted from the crystal chandelier overhead to the carefully curated collection of Renaissance art adorning the walls.

"The original house dates back to the seventeenth century," Bernard explained, his hand resting lightly on the small of Shaniece's back. "Though we've made some modern improvements over the years."

Tanya watched her mother lean into his touch, a soft smile playing across her face. The intimacy of the gesture made her chest tighten with an emotion she couldn't quite name.

"The gardens are particularly lovely this time of year." Bernard gestured through the floor-to-ceiling windows. "Perhaps we could take our aperitifs on the terrace?"

Aperitifs, Tanya thought. *Who the fuck uses those kind of words?*

"That sounds perfect, darling," Shaniece's voice carried a warmth Tanya had never heard before.

They stepped out onto the limestone terrace where a butler had already set up a small table with champagne and delicate canapés. The manicured gardens stretched out before them, roses climbing ancient stone walls and boxwood hedges creating intimate green rooms.

"I understand you're quite successful in the art world," Bernard said, handing Tanya a crystal flute of champagne. His green eyes crinkled at the corners when he smiled. "I'd love to hear your thoughts on some pieces I've recently acquired."

"I specialize in contemporary artists, particularly emerging talents of color," Tanya took a careful sip, noting how the vintage champagne danced on her tongue. "Though I appreciate classical works as well."

"Your Mama mentioned you helped her build her art collection," Bernard's use of the familiar term caught Tanya off guard. The way he said it - with such genuine affection - made something shift in her perception of him.

Shaniece laughed, reaching for Bernard's hand. "He's being modest. Bernard's family has been collecting art for generations. The pieces in his study would make museum curators weep."

"Speaking of which..." Bernard squeezed Shaniece's fingers. "Would you like to see it, Tanya? I have a particular piece I think might interest you."

As they walked through the villa's winding corridors, Tanya couldn't help but notice how naturally her mother fit into this world of old money and refined taste. Shaniece's burgundy wrap dress complemented the deep woods and rich textiles of their surroundings—as if she'd always belonged there.

Bernard's study proved to be a testament to generations of careful collecting. Dark wooden bookshelves reached toward coffered ceilings, while strategically placed spotlights illuminated various artworks. But what caught Tanya's attention was the way Bernard pulled out her mother's chair before seating himself, the casual tenderness with which he touched her shoulder as he passed.

"This is my favorite room in the house," Shaniece confided, her eyes bright. "Bernard and I spent hours in here when we first met, just talking about art and life."

"And falling in love," Bernard added softly, his accent wrapping around the words like silk.

Tanya watched them share a look that felt almost too intimate to witness. For the first time since hearing about their engagement, she saw past the whirlwind romance to something deeper. The way they moved in sync, finished each other's thoughts, traded secret smiles - it spoke of a connection that transcended their short time together.

"You know, Tanya," Bernard turned to her, his expression earnest,

"Shaniece has told me so much about you. I hope you'll give me the chance to be part of your family."

The sincerity in his voice made Tanya's carefully constructed walls waver. She glanced at her mother, saw the mixture of hope and love shining in her eyes, and felt her skepticism begin to crack.

* * *

THE TERRACE OVERLOOKED SPRAWLING gardens that stretched toward distant hills painted gold by the setting sun. Tanya sank into a plush cushioned chair, accepting a crystal flute of champagne from Bernard. The bubbles tickled her nose as she watched her mother and Bernard settle into a loveseat, their bodies angled toward each other with easy intimacy.

"I must apologize again for my son's absence," Bernard checked his phone. "He takes his responsibilities very seriously—perhaps too seriously sometimes."

"Just like his father," Shaniece said, her hand finding Bernard's knee.

"Tonight at dinner you'll meet a few of my cousins as well," Bernard added, kissing air towards her Mama.

Tanya studied the way Bernard's expression softened at her mother's touch. The tenderness in his green eyes held none of the calculation or hidden agenda she'd feared to find. Her shoulders relaxed a fraction.

"Tell me more about the restoration work you mentioned," Tanya said, genuinely curious about the property's history. "These gardens are incredible."

Bernard's face lit up. "Ah, yes. This estate has been in my family since the time of Louis XIV. Those rose gardens were originally planted by my great-great-grandmother Adelaide." He gestured toward a formal garden bordered by perfectly trimmed hedges. "She was quite the revolutionary for her time—insisted on managing the grounds herself rather than leaving it to the gardeners."

"Which explains where your son gets his determination," Shaniece added with a knowing smile.

"Indeed," Bernard chuckled. "Though I like to think he inherited some of my business sense as well. He's been instrumental in modernizing our company's approach to sustainable development."

The pride in Bernard's voice when he spoke of his son was unmistakable. Tanya found herself wondering what kind of man could inspire such obvious paternal admiration.

A server appeared with a tray of delicate canapés. Tanya selected one topped with smoked salmon and fresh dill, savoring the blend of flavors as Bernard continued sharing family stories. His animated descriptions of childhood adventures in these gardens painted a picture of a home filled with love and tradition.

"And this spot right here," Bernard said, indicating the terrace where they sat, "is where my father taught me to play chess. We would spend hours here, discussing everything from philosophy to business strategy over the board."

"Now I understand where you developed your tactical thinking," Shaniece teased.

"Which you saw right through, my dear." Bernard brought her hand to his lips.

Tanya's chest tightened at their easy affection. The man before her bore no resemblance to the cold, calculating aristocrat she'd imagined when her mother first announced their engagement. Instead, Bernard radiated genuine warmth and consideration.

The sky deepened to dusky purple as they talked, lights automatically illuminating the gardens in a soft golden glow. A cool breeze carried the sweet scent of jasmine from climbing vines nearby. Tanya found herself relaxing into the peaceful atmosphere, her earlier misgivings fading with each passing moment.

"Your vision for updating the property while preserving its character is fascinating," she said, genuinely impressed by Bernard's plans. "The solar integration sounds particularly innovative."

"That was my son's suggestion, actually," Bernard's eyes crinkled with pride. "He has quite the eye for blending traditional architecture with modern sustainability practices—oh, here he is now."

the wedding prep

. . .

Tanya's heart kept a steady rhythm until Bernard's proud voice cut through the evening air. "I'm delighted to introduce my son, Alexandre."

Her fingers tightened around the stem of her wine glass as familiar footsteps clicked against the marble floor. The world tilted on its axis when she lifted her gaze to meet striking blue eyes - the same ones that had sparkled with desire in the dim light of that wine bar just last evening.

Alexandre's confident stride carried him forward, but Tanya caught the slight hesitation in his step when their eyes locked. His hand extended toward Shaniece first, his voice warm and controlled. "A pleasure to finally meet you. My father speaks of nothing else these days."

The sound of his voice—that perfect blend of French accent and polished English—sent a jolt through Tanya's system. Her mind flashed to whispered words against bare skin, to fingertips tracing paths in darkness.

"And this is my daughter, Tanya," Shaniece's voice pulled her back to the present moment.

Alexandre turned to her, his expression a masterpiece of composure save for the slight tightening around his eyes. "Enchanted, mademoiselle."

His hand clasped hers in a formal greeting, but the touch sparked with memories of how those same fingers had tangled in her hair, traced the curve of her spine. Tanya managed a slight shake of her head, a silent plea in her eyes.

He caught her meaning instantly, releasing her hand with perfect social grace. "Father tells me you're quite accomplished in the art world. I'd love to hear more about your gallery."

Bernard clapped his hands together, pride radiating from his features. "Alexandre has quite an eye for art—but before we get into that discussion..." He placed a hand on his son's shoulder. "Come, I need your input on some business matters we discussed earlier."

Alexandre inclined his head in a polite nod to both women. "If you'll excuse us. We won't be long."

Tanya watched them disappear into Bernard's study, her pulse still racing beneath her careful exterior. The garden air felt too thick, too close to her skin.

"Tanya?" Shaniece's concerned voice cut through her spiral. "Baby, you look like you've seen a ghost. What's wrong?"

"I'm fine, Mama." The words came out steadier than she felt. Her gaze fixed on a distant point in the garden, avoiding her mother's searching eyes. "Just... surprised, I guess."

Shaniece stepped closer, her perfume carrying the familiar comfort of home. "I know this is all happening fast. But

Alexandre seems lovely, doesn't he? Good-looking ... just like his father."

A hysterical laugh threatened to bubble up from Tanya's chest. *Lovely*. If her mother only knew how *lovely* she'd already found him.

"Listen," Shaniece squeezed her arm gently, "why don't we focus on something else? The wedding preparations still need attention. We could look at the flower arrangements I've been considering."

Tanya hesitated, her mind still reeling from the collision of her past indiscretion with her present reality. But her mother's suggestion offered an escape route from the chaos of her thoughts. She nodded, grateful for the distraction. "Yes, let's do that."

* * *

THE LATE AFTERNOON sun cast long shadows across the manicured lawn as Tanya followed her mother down the stone path. Her heels clicked against the weathered pavement, each step bringing them closer to the gazebo atrium where Shaniece would soon marry Bernard.

"The florist suggested white peonies mixed with deep burgundy roses." Shaniece's hands danced through the air, painting invisible arrangements. "What do you think, baby? Too classic?"

Tanya's attention drifted toward the main house, its limestone facade gleaming in the golden light. Somewhere behind those walls, Alexandre was speaking with his father. The same Alexandre who had traced constellations on her skin just hours ago. Her stomach twisted into knots at the memory.

"Tanya?" Shaniece's voice cut through her thoughts. "You're a million miles away."

"Sorry, Mama. The peonies sound perfect." She turned her head once more, scanning the upper windows. A shadow moved behind one of them, and her pulse quickened before she realized it was just a maid drawing the curtains.

"And I thought we could hang crystal chandeliers from the gazebo rafters." Shaniece continued walking, her designer heels navigating the path with practiced ease. "The wedding planner says they'll catch the sunset just right."

Another glance backward. This time, Tanya caught sight of Bernard's assistant directing caterers through the kitchen entrance. But no Alexandre. The anticipation of seeing him again, of having to maintain this charade of strangers, made her skin prickle with nervous energy.

The gazebo rose before them, its white-painted wood gleaming against the backdrop of perfectly trimmed hedges. Shaniece ascended the steps, her face lighting up as she gestured to different corners of the space.

"The string quartet will set up here," she indicated the left side. "And the officiant will stand beneath this arch." Her fingers traced the wooden trellis where climbing roses would soon bloom.

Tanya forced her attention to the present moment, to her mother's joy. She pulled her lips into what she hoped was a convincing smile. "It's going to be beautiful, Mama."

"These columns will be wrapped in silk ribbons." Shaniece moved from post to post, her enthusiasm building. "And lanterns will hang from every corner."

But even as Tanya nodded and made appropriate sounds of appreciation, her thoughts kept circling back to Alexandre. To the way his eyes had widened in recognition. To the silent agreement that had passed between them in that fraction of a second. To the weight of secrets that now pressed against her chest.

"And here's where you'll stand as my maid of honor." Shaniece patted the spot to her left, her eyes growing misty. "I never thought I'd have this, baby. A real fairy tale wedding."

The word 'fairy tale' stuck in Tanya's throat. *What kind of fairy tale included sleeping with your future stepbrother before knowing who he was?* She swallowed hard and focused on a point just past her mother's shoulder, where garden workers were installing strings of market lights between the trees.

"I know it's fast," Shaniece continued, mistaking Tanya's distraction for concern. "But when you know, you just know. Don't you think?"

The question hung in the air between them, heavy with implications Tanya wasn't ready to face. She busied herself straightening a loose board on the gazebo railing, buying time before she had to respond. In the distance, a door opened and closed, drawing her attention back to the house once more.

The afternoon light softened as Bernard and Alexandre made their way down the cobbled path. Tanya's heart hammered against her ribs as she watched them approach, Alexandre's long strides matching his father's purposeful gait.

"The flowers will cascade down these columns," Bernard's voice carried across the garden as they drew closer. He gestured broadly at the gazebo's structure. "Like a waterfall of white and burgundy."

Shaniece beamed at her fiancé. "I was just telling Tanya about the arrangements."

"Forty-eight years," Bernard wrapped an arm around Shaniece's waist. "That's how long I've waited to find the perfect woman to share this place with. And now, my darling, we'll fill it with memories of our own."

Alexandre shifted his weight, his blue eyes darting between Tanya and the ground. "Father, perhaps Miss Washington would like to see the rose garden while you and Shaniece finish discussing the wedding details?"

Tanya's fingers curled into her palms. The formal way he said her name felt like a slap.

"Wonderful idea," Bernard nodded. "The roses are particularly lovely this time of year."

Before Tanya could protest, Alexandre had already started walking toward the eastern path. She followed, her heels sinking slightly into the manicured grass as they rounded a high hedge that blocked them from view.

The moment they were alone, Alexandre whirled around. "Je n'en crois pas mes yeux! C'est complètement fou!" His voice cracked with emotion. "I cannot believe it's you! What madness is this?"

"Keep your voice down," Tanya hissed, glancing back toward the gazebo.

"Did you know?" His accent thickened with anger. "When you came to my bed, did you know who I was?"

Heat rushed to Tanya's face. "How dare you? You think I orchestrated this?" She stepped closer, jabbing a finger at his chest. "I came to Paris to stop my mother from making a mistake, not to seduce my future stepbrother!"

"Stepbrother?" Alexandre's face contorted. "Mon Dieu, I hadn't even thought of that yet."

"Well, congratulations on catching up," Tanya's voice dripped with sarcasm. "And for the record, you came to *my* bed, not the other way around."

"I didn't hear any complaints last night." His eyes flashed dangerously.

"Because I didn't know who you were!" She threw her hands up in frustration. "This is insane. You're insane for even suggesting I planned this."

"What am I supposed to think?" He ran his fingers through his hair. "You show up at my father's engagement dinner, after disappearing without a word—"

"Oh, like you were planning to call?" Tanya cut him off. "You snuck out before dawn!"

"Because that's what one does after a one-night stand!" His voice rose again. "Which was clearly all it was meant to be, n'est-ce pas?"

"Yes, exactly!" Tanya's chest heaved with anger. "A one-time mistake that never should have happened!"

Alexandre stepped back as if she'd struck him. "Très bien. Then we are in agreement. It never happened."

"Fine by me!"

"Fine!"

Tanya spun on her heel, nearly twisting her ankle in the soft grass as she stormed back toward the house. Behind her, she heard Alexandre's footsteps heading in the opposite direction, followed by the sharp crack of a branch being kicked out of his path.

alexandre

...

I stand rooted to the spot, my carefully cultivated composure threatening to crack. The universe must be playing some cruel joke. There she is - the woman who's haunted my thoughts since that night at the wine bar - standing in my family's garden, looking just as stunning in daylight as she did in the dim bar lighting.

"Alexandre, won't you come say hello properly?" My Papa's voice cuts through my shocked daze.

My feet move automatically, years of social training taking over while my mind races. She's wearing a cream silk blouse that catches the sunlight, her locs swept up elegantly. Just hours ago, those same locs had been spread across my pillow. Now she's here, about to become my... step-sister? The thought makes my stomach lurch.

"Enchanté," I manage, extending my hand to Shaniece first, buying precious seconds before I have to face her daughter. "Welcome to our home."

When I finally turn to Tanya, her face is a masterpiece of controlled panic. Our handshake is brief, formal, both of us pulling away as if burned. Her skin is just as soft as I remember.

"Pleasure to meet you," she says evenly, but I catch a slight tremor in her voice.

I make some inane comment about the weather, watching her throat work as she swallows hard. All I can think about is how I'd traced that elegant neck with my lips, how she'd gasped when I'd...

BACK IN MY ROOM, I pace like a caged animal. Five steps to the window, pivot, five steps back. My normally ordered thoughts are chaos. That night had been perfect precisely because it was supposed to be temporary - a beautiful stranger, a passionate connection, no strings attached. Now those non-existent strings are suddenly steel cables binding our families together.

I stop at the window, pressing my forehead against the cool glass. Below, I can see Tanya and Shaniece walking through the garden, my Papa pointing out various features of the estate. Tanya's head is bent toward her mother, but I can read the tension in her shoulders even from here.

"Merde," I mutter, pushing away from the window. My carefully controlled life is spiraling into a soap opera plot. I've built my reputation on sound judgment and strategic thinking. But there's no strategic solution to this mess that doesn't end in someone getting hurt.

The rational part of my brain starts cataloging options. We could pretend we've never met - but one slip, one unguarded moment could shatter the facade. We could confess everything now - but that would devastate our parents during what should be their happiest time. Or we could...

I sink onto the edge of my bed ... a bed where just last night... No. I can't think about that now. I need to focus on damage control. But every time I try to think logically, all I can remember is the way she'd looked at me across that bar, the spark in her eyes when she'd suggested we leave together.

My Papa's study is just down the hall. I should go to him now, be honest before this situation becomes even more complicated. The longer we wait, the worse it will be. I stand up, straighten my tie, and take three steps toward the door before stopping again.

"Comment je vais expliquer ça?" I mutter to myself, running both hands through my hair in frustration. How do I even begin to explain this to my Papa?

I resume my pacing, each step on the Persian carpet echoing my racing thoughts. The smooth wood panels of my childhood bedroom mock me with their familiarity - how many times had I hidden here to escape uncomfortable situations? But never one quite like this.

My hands won't stay still. I clench them, unclench them, run them through my hair until I must look as disheveled as I feel. The mirror catches my reflection - I barely recognize myself. Gone is the composed businessman who closes million-euro deals without breaking a sweat. In his place stands a man who looks like he's seen a ghost. Or rather, the woman he'd left in bed that morning, only to materialize in his family's garden.

What are my options? Tell Papa everything? "By the way, Papa, I had a magnificent one-night stand with your fiancée's daughter before I knew who she was." *Brilliant. Or perhaps maintain this charade of strangers? But for how long? Through family dinners, holidays, celebrations?*

The weight of every possible scenario crashes down on me. I could leave - cite urgent business in London or Dubai. But that would only delay the inevitable. And running away has never been my style.

My feet carry me to the door. Maybe if I catch Papa alone, explain things carefully...

The heavy oak door swings open before I can reach for it. Papa stands there, his brow furrowed with concern. "Alexandre? Why are you hiding up here? Everyone's gathering for dinner."

"Papa, I..." The words stick in my throat. I study his face - the happiness that's been radiating from him since he met Shaniece. *How can I taint that with this mess?*

"Is it business troubles?" He steps into the room, closing the door behind him. "The Shanghai development?"

A perfect excuse presents itself. I could blame work stress, buy myself time to figure this out. But lying to my Papa feels wrong. We've always been honest with each other, especially since Maman passed.

"Non, the business is fine," I straighten my tie, an automatic gesture. "I just needed a moment to... collect my thoughts."

"You seem distracted." He places a hand on my shoulder, his touch steady and familiar. "Are you sure there's nothing you want to tell me?"

Everything in me screams to confess, to share this burden. But I look at his kind eyes, picture the joy on his face when he introduces Shaniece to our relatives, and I can't do it. Not now. Not like this.

"I'll be down in a minute," I manage, forcing a smile. "Just give me a moment to freshen up."

He studies me for another second, and I wonder if he can see through my attempted composure. But then he nods, squeezing my shoulder before turning to leave.

"Don't take too long. Shaniece's daughter seems lovely - I think you two will get along well."

The irony of his words hits me like a physical blow. If he only knew how well we'd already gotten along.

The door closes behind him with a soft click, leaving me alone again with my thoughts and the memory of Tanya's shocked expression in the garden.

I stumble into my en-suite bathroom, flicking on the lights with trembling fingers. The marble countertop feels cool under my palms as I lean over the sink, staring at my reflection. Is this really happening? The face looking back at me seems foreign - gone is my usual controlled expression, replaced by wide eyes and a complexion several shades paler than normal.

Cold water splashes against my skin as I cup my hands under the faucet. The shock of it does nothing to clear my head. If anything, the icy sensation reminds me of how Tanya had traced her cold fingertips down my chest last night, sending shivers through my body.

"Merde, merde, merde," I mutter, grabbing a hand towel and pressing it against my face. The Egyptian cotton feels rough against my skin, and I realize my nerves are completely shot. Every sensation seems heightened, overwhelming.

The bathroom suddenly feels too small, too confined. The shower in the corner mocks me - I'd taken an extra-long one this morning, trying to wash away the lingering scent of her perfume. Now that same perfume will probably become a regular presence in this house. At family dinners. During holidays. At the wedding...

My stomach lurches at the thought of the wedding. I'll have to stand there, watching my father marry her mother, pretending I've never seen Tanya naked, never heard her gasp under my weight, never...

"Stop it," I growl at my reflection. This line of thinking isn't helping. I need solutions, not memories.

The obvious answer would be to leave. I have properties to inspect in London, meetings I could schedule in Dubai, deals to close in Singapore. I could be on a plane within hours, citing urgent business. It wouldn't even be a lie - there's always urgent business somewhere in our global portfolio.

I pace the length of the bathroom, five steps there, five steps back. The sound of my Italian leather shoes on the marble tiles echoes off the walls, matching the pounding in my head. Running away would be cowardly, but isn't it better than facing this impossible situation?

Through the bathroom window, I catch glimpses of the garden. Voices drift up - laughter, the clink of glasses, the sounds of my family preparing for dinner. Papa's deep chuckle mingles with Shaniece's melodious laugh. They sound so happy, so right together.

And here I am, hiding in my bathroom like a teenager, all because I can't face the woman I left in a hotel room this morning. The woman who's about to become my step-sister. The woman whose touch I can still feel on my skin.

I splash more cold water on my face, not caring that droplets are falling on my custom-made shirt. The water does nothing to wash away the memory of her lips against mine, the way she'd whispered "fuck me" in the dark, how perfectly she'd fit in my arms...

My reflection shows a man coming undone. My carefully styled hair is a mess from running my hands through it. My tie hangs loose around my neck. I look nothing like the composed businessman who closes multi-million euro deals without breaking a sweat.

A knock at my bedroom door makes me jump. "Alexandre?" Papa's voice calls out. "Everyone's waiting."

I grip the edge of the sink harder, my knuckles turning white. The thought of sitting across from Tanya at dinner, making polite conversation while pretending we're strangers... It's unbearable. Maybe if I claim a sudden migraine? Food poisoning? Anything to avoid going downstairs.

But I know I can't hide forever. Eventually, I'll have to face her, face this situation we've created. The longer I wait, the more suspicious it will seem. Already, my absence must be raising questions.

"Just a minute!" I call back, my voice sounding strained even to my own ears. I straighten my tie with trembling fingers, trying to reconstruct my usual polished appearance. But it feels like putting on a costume, playing a part in some absurd farce.

The sound of footsteps retreating from my door provides momentary relief. But it's short-lived as I realize each passing minute brings me closer to an inevitable confrontation. The thought of those amber eyes meeting mine across the dinner table makes my chest tight.

tanya
. . .

I stand beside Mama, our fingers intertwined as guests filter into the engagement dinner. My palm is sweaty against hers, but I can't let go. She's my anchor in this surreal moment, even though she has no idea why I'm gripping her hand like a lifeline.

"Isn't this beautiful, baby?" Mama's eyes sparkle as she takes in the twinkling lights strung across the garden terrace. "Bernard thought of everything."

I manage what I hope passes for an enthusiastic nod, but my thoughts are scattered like the rose petals dotting the cobblestones. The string quartet's melody floats through the air, mixing with the gentle splash of the fountain and the lyrical flow of French conversation around us. Everything feels dreamlike, yet razor-sharp real.

My gaze keeps drifting to Alexandre despite my best efforts. He's across the terrace, deep in conversation with an elderly couple, his tailored suit highlighting every inch of the body I'd explored just last night. The memory makes heat flood my cheeks, and I quickly look away when he glances in my direction.

This can't be happening. The sophisticated Frenchman who'd kissed me senseless against my hotel room door is about to become my step-brother. *The universe must be laughing its ass off right now.*

"Tanya?" Mama's voice breaks through my spiral. "You're crushing my hand, sweetie."

I release her fingers immediately, flexing my own. "Sorry, Mama. Just... taking it all in."

But the implications keep hitting me in waves. Every family dinner. Every holiday. Every milestone celebration - he'll be there. The man who'd whispered French endearments against my skin will sit across from me at Sunday brunch. My chest constricts at the thought.

The chatter around us fades to white noise as my breathing quickens. The perfectly manicured garden starts to spin slightly. I need air, which is ridiculous since we're already outside.

"I'm going to get some water," I tell Mama, already backing away. She's immediately swept into a conversation with Bernard's cousin, and I slip through the crowd of guests.

I find a quiet spot against the villa's limestone wall, pressing my palms against the cool stone. The lavender bushes nearby release their soothing scent with each evening breeze, but even that can't calm my racing thoughts.

My carefully ordered world has transformed into some twisted romantic comedy, except I'm not laughing. I close my eyes, trying to center myself through the breathing exercises my therapist taught me. In through the nose, out through the mouth. Focus on the present moment.

But the present moment is the problem. Alexandre is the problem. The heat of his gaze when our eyes meet across rooms, the memory of his touch - it's all too much.

I press my back against the rough stone wall, grateful for its solid presence as my chest tightens. The string quartet's melody fades, replaced by the thundering of my pulse in my ears. Black spots dance at the edges of my vision. *Not here. Not now.* But my body isn't listening to reason.

My heels click against the limestone steps as I stumble further down the garden path, away from the lights and laughter. The thick hedges and towering cypress trees create a natural barrier between me and the party above. Here, in this secluded spot, I can fall apart without an audience.

The sweet scent of jasmine wraps around me like a comfort blanket. I've always found peace in gardens - probably because Mama used to take me to the Chicago Botanic Garden whenever money was tight and we needed a free adventure. We'd make up stories about the flowers, pretend we were fairy princesses in our own magical kingdom.

But there's no pretending my way out of this mess.

I tilt my head back, focusing on the vast expanse of indigo sky above. The stars look different here in the French countryside, clearer and more numerous than back home. They twinkle against the darkness like scattered diamonds, steady and unchanging despite my world spinning out of control below.

Breathe in for four counts. The crisp evening air fills my lungs.

Hold for seven. My racing thoughts begin to slow.

Out for eight. Some of the tension leaves my shoulders.

The gravel crunches beneath my feet as I shift my weight, bracing my hands on my knees. Another deep breath. The sweet-spicy fragrance of roses mingles with lavender and thyme from Bernard's herb garden. It grounds me in the present moment, even as my mind tries to spiral into worst-case scenarios.

What would Mama say if she knew? The thought sends another wave of anxiety through me. She's so happy, practically glowing with joy every time Bernard looks at her. I've never seen her like this - not with any of the few men she dated while raising me. She deserves this happiness.

But her daughter hooking up with her fiancé's son? That would devastate her.

Breathe in. The climbing wisteria forms a delicate canopy overhead, its pale blooms ghostly in the starlight.

Hold. A gentle breeze carries the distant sound of clinking glasses and muted laughter.

Release. My heartbeat finally begins to steady.

This garden feels ancient, like it's seen centuries of human drama unfold beneath these same stars. *How many others have hidden in these shadows, wrestling with their own impossible situations?* The thought is oddly comforting. My problems suddenly seem smaller against the backdrop of this timeless space.

I close my eyes, letting the peace of the garden wash over me. The stone steps are cool beneath me as I sink down to sit, not caring about my designer dress anymore. The rhythmic chirping of crickets creates a gentle melody, so different from Chicago's constant urban hum.

My breathing syncs with the natural rhythm of the garden - the rustle of leaves, the distant fountain's splash, the soft night sounds of birds settling in their nests. Each inhale brings clarity, each exhale carries away a fraction of my panic.

I can handle this. I *have* to handle this. For Mama's sake, if nothing else. Alexandre and I are adults. We can be mature about this situation, keep our distance, pretend that night never happened. It's not like I was planning on a relationship anyway - Paris flings are supposed to stay in Paris, right?

The mantra feels hollow even as I think it, but I cling to it anyway. It's the only way forward I can see right now.

A tear escapes despite my best efforts. I swipe it away quickly, smudging my carefully applied makeup. *Pull it together, Tanya.* Your mother needs you to be strong right now. This is her moment.

I straighten my shoulders and smooth down my dress. One more deep breath, and I plaster on my best gallery-opening smile. Time to go be the supportive daughter my mother deserves.

My heel catches between the limestone steps as I freeze mid-stride. Alexandre stands three stairs above me, his hands sliding into his pockets in that distinctly European way. The party sounds fade to white noise, leaving only the fountain's gentle splash and chirping crickets between us.

His blue eyes lock with mine, and suddenly I'm back in that wine bar, caught in his magnetic pull. The same electricity crackles in the air, but now it's tangled with complications I couldn't have imagined twenty-four hours ago.

My fingers grip the iron railing, its cool metal grounding me. Alexandre hasn't moved, his tall frame silhouetted against the garden lights above. His jaw clenches slightly - the same way it did when he'd whispered French endearments against my neck. The memory sends an unwanted shiver down my spine.

The jasmine-scented breeze rustles through the cypress trees, carrying the distant melody of the string quartet. It's surreal how everything keeps moving forward while we're frozen in this moment, trapped between what was and what can never be.

My curator's eye can't help but notice how he fits perfectly into this setting - the elegant French garden, the historic villa, the twinkling lights. His tailored suit jacket stretches across broad shoulders I'd raked my nails down just hours ago. The thought makes my cheeks burn.

Time stretches like honey, thick and sweet and suspended. A thousand words hover between us—explanations, apologies, possibilities—but none make it past my lips. *What could I possibly say? "Thanks for the mind-blowing sex, future step-brother"?*

His fingers flex in his pockets, and I catch the slight tremor in his hands before they disappear deeper into the fine wool of his trousers. So he's not as composed as he appears. The realization brings an odd comfort - at least I'm not alone in my turmoil.

A burst of laughter from the party above makes me flinch. It breaks our eye contact for a split second, but when our gazes meet again, the intensity has doubled. There's heat there, barely banked desire, but also something deeper - regret maybe, or resignation.

My heart pounds against my ribs so hard I wonder if he can hear it echoing off the limestone walls. The steps feel unsteady beneath my feet, though I haven't moved an inch. One of us should say something, do something, break this charged silence before it suffocates us both.

But words seem inadequate for this moment. What language could possibly capture the cosmic joke of falling into bed with your future step-brother? My high school French certainly isn't up to the task, and English feels too harsh for the delicate complexity of our situation.

A light breeze lifts a strand of hair across my face. Alexandre's fingers twitch in his pockets, and I know he's fighting the urge to reach out and brush it away.

Now we stand frozen on these ancient steps, while above us our parents celebrate their love story. The irony isn't lost on me - how their fairy tale romance has twisted mine into something impossible before it could even begin.

The wing of a moth brushes my bare shoulder, drawn to the garden lights. I envy its simple existence, governed by pure instinct without the messy complications of family dynamics and social expectations. It flutters between us, casting tiny shadows on the limestone, before disappearing into the darkness beyond.

Still, neither of us speaks. The silence has become its own entity, heavy with unspoken desires and impossible choices. My lips part slightly, but I swallow the words before they can escape. What's the point? Any path forward from this moment leads to pain - for us, for our parents, for this newly forming family.

The fountain keeps its steady rhythm, counting heartbeats in liquid silver. Alexandre shifts his weight slightly, the gravel crunching beneath his Italian leather shoes. The sound seems to echo through the garden, though it's barely louder than a whisper.

We're close enough that I can smell his cologne - the same scent that clung to my skin this morning. It mingles with the garden's perfume, creating something new and bittersweet. Like everything else about this moment, it's both beautiful and painful.

limestone steps
. . .

The limestone steps felt cool beneath Tanya as she settled onto them, the ancient stone worn smooth by generations of footsteps. Beside her, Alexandre's presence radiated warmth, a stark contrast to the evening chill seeping through her black dress.

Alexandre cleared his throat, breaking the heavy silence between them. "We need to discuss what we're going to do about this." His French accent wrapped around the words, making them sound both elegant and final. "I plan to tell Papa the truth."

"Your father?" Tanya shifted, turning to face him. The fading twilight caught his profile, highlighting the determined set of his jaw.

"I've never kept secrets from him." Alexandre's blue eyes met hers, searching. "Our relationship is built on honesty. This..." He gestured between them. "This feels wrong to hide."

Tanya's chest tightened as she thought of her Mama. They'd shared everything since she was little - homework struggles, first crushes, career victories. The weight of this secret already felt like a stone in her stomach.

"I understand," she said softly. "Mama and I... we don't do secrets either. Not since..." She trailed off, remembering how they'd supported each other after her father left.

Alexandre ran a hand through his hair, mussing the careful styling. "This situation - it's maddening. The timing, the circumstances..." His voice dropped lower. "The way I can't stop thinking about that night."

Heat bloomed across Tanya's cheeks. The memory of their shared passion flickered between them, electric and undeniable. "I know," she whispered.

"I love Papa," Alexandre continued. "I see how happy he is with your mother. The thought of causing them pain..." He shook his head, frustration evident in every movement.

"That's exactly it," Tanya wrapped her arms around herself. "Mama deserves this happiness. After everything she's been through, raising me alone, working so hard..." She blinked back sudden tears. "I hate lying to her."

They stood in silence for a moment, the garden's ambient sounds filling the space between them - distant laughter from the party, the gentle splash of the fountain, birds settling in for the evening.

"Perhaps," Alexandre said carefully, "we wait until after the wedding."

Tanya nodded slowly. "Give them their moment."

"Let them have their celebration without complications."

A small, bittersweet smile curved Tanya's lips. "It makes sense." The decision felt right, even as it added to the complexity of their situation.

"We'll tell them afterward," Alexandre assured her. "Complete honesty."

"Complete honesty," Tanya agreed, feeling some of the tension release from her shoulders.

Alexandre reached for her hand, his fingers warm against hers. The simple touch sent sparks racing up her arm, reminding her that their attraction hadn't diminished despite the complications.

"Ready to head back?" he asked, his thumb tracing circles on her palm.

"Almost," Tanya allowed herself to enjoy the moment of connection. They exchanged soft smiles, both aware that their journey was just beginning.

The garden's evening shadows deepened around them as Tanya stared at their joined hands. Her heart thundered against her ribs, each beat a warning she struggled to heed. Alexandre's fingers were warm against her palm, his touch sending familiar sparks of electricity racing through her body.

The memory of their night together flashed hot in her mind - his hands mapping her skin, his lips trailing fire down her throat. Heat bloomed across her chest and neck. She shifted on the limestone step, hyper-aware of how close they sat, their thighs nearly touching.

Alexandre's thumb continued its maddening circles on her palm. The gentle pressure made her breath catch, awakening every nerve ending. His cologne - that same intoxicating blend of citrus and cedar that had first drawn her in at the wine bar - wrapped around her senses.

Tanya's gaze drifted to his mouth, remembering how those lips had felt against hers, how they'd curved into a smile between kisses. Her body hummed with the need to close the distance between them, to taste him again. The urge was so strong her muscles tensed with the effort of staying still.

He was right there. So close. All she had to do was lean in...

The thought jolted her back to reality. *What was she doing?* They'd just agreed to keep things quiet until after the wedding. Starting something now would only complicate everything further.

Tanya yanked her hand from his grip, wrapping both arms tightly around her middle. Her fingers itched to reach for him, to slide into his hair and pull him down for a kiss that would erase all their careful plans. She locked her arms in place, pressing them hard against her ribs.

The loss of contact left her skin tingling. She could feel Alexandre's eyes on her, probably questioning her sudden withdrawal. But she didn't dare look at him. Not when her control felt so fragile, balanced on a knife's edge of desire and common sense.

Her body remembered exactly how it felt to be pressed against his, how perfectly they'd fit together. The memory pulsed through her blood, making her fingers dig deeper into her sides. She needed this physical restraint to keep from reaching for him.

God, why did he have to smell so good? Why did every subtle movement of his body have to draw her attention like a magnet? The sophisticated cut of his suit only emphasized his athletic build, making her remember how it felt to run her hands over those shoulders, down that chest...

Tanya squeezed her eyes shut, trying to block out the images flooding her mind. This was insane. She was sitting here literally hugging herself to keep from jumping the man who was about to become her step-brother. The absurdity of the situation might have made her laugh if she wasn't so overwhelmed by want.

The cool evening air did nothing to calm the heat burning under her skin. She could hear Alexandre's steady breathing beside her, feel the weight of his presence like a physical touch. Every molecule between them seemed charged with potential energy, just waiting for a spark.

The rational part of her brain screamed warnings about boundaries, complications, and family dynamics. But her body remembered the skillful touch of his hands, the perfect pressure of his kisses, the way he'd made her feel more alive than she'd ever been.

She pressed her arms tighter around herself, using the pressure to ground her thoughts. Focus on breathing. Focus on anything except how badly she wanted to turn and crash her lips against his. Focus on why that would be a terrible idea right now.

The garden's peace felt like a mockery. Nothing about this situation was peaceful. Not when every cell in her body strained toward him like a flower seeking the sun. Not when keeping her hands locked around her waist felt like the hardest thing she'd ever done.

* * *

ALEXANDRE WATCHED as Tanya pulled her hand from his, an ache spreading through his palm at the loss of contact. She wrapped her arms tightly around her waist, a gesture that only emphasized the elegant curve of her body. His fingers twitched with the urge to reach for her again.

God, he wanted her. The need coursed through his veins like wildfire, threatening to consume his carefully maintained control. Images from their night together flashed through his mind - her soft moans, the way she'd arched beneath him, how perfectly their bodies had moved together. His muscles tensed with the effort of staying seated beside her on the limestone steps.

The garden wall loomed just feet away, its ancient stones weathered smooth by centuries of rain. It would be so easy to guide her there, to press her against that cool surface and claim her mouth with his. To slide his hands along her sides, drawing those incredible sounds from her throat again. His breath caught at the thought.

Their chemistry crackled in the space between them, electric and undeniable. He could feel it humming beneath his skin, making every nerve ending spark with awareness. The sophisticated façade he typically wore felt paper-thin, ready to tear apart under the force of his desire.

His gaze dropped to her lips, lingering on their full curve. They were slightly parted as she took shallow breaths, and he remembered exactly how they'd felt against his - soft, eager, demanding. The memory of their kisses burned through him. He wanted to taste her again, to take her mouth in a kiss that would leave them both breathless and aching for more.

Last night played on repeat in his mind - the way she'd melted into his touch, how she'd moaned in his ear, the incredible feeling of being completely lost in her. His body responded instantly to the memories, making his tailored trousers uncomfortably tight. *Would she want that again? Would she let him worship every inch of her skin, draw gasps and sighs from those tempting lips?*

The questions circled his mind like hungry wolves, but he kept them locked behind clenched teeth. They'd just agreed to keep things quiet until after the wedding. Propositioning her now would only complicate their already messy situation. Still, his hands gripped his thighs hard enough to leave marks, the physical restraint necessary to keep from reaching for her.

The rising moon painted blue highlights in her hair, making her skin glow. Every slight movement drew his attention - the rise and fall of her chest, the nervous tap of her fingers against her ribs, the way she worried her bottom lip between her teeth. She was the most beautiful torture he'd ever encountered.

The sophisticated man he presented to the world - the successful businessman, the dutiful son - felt like a distant memory. In this moment, he was pure wanting, stripped down to base instinct by her mere presence. His heart thundered against his ribs, each beat screaming for him to close the distance between them, consequences be damned.

But he remained still, letting the evening air cool his heated skin. Even as his body thrummed with need, even as every muscle strained toward her, he kept his position on the step. The physical distance between them felt like miles and millimeters at the same time - too far to satisfy, too close to think clearly.

au revoir, ma belle

. . .

A week later

The Dubois estate bloomed with roses and hydrangeas. White chairs dotted the emerald lawn around the gazebo where Bernard and Shaniece exchanged their vows beneath a canopy of wisteria. Tanya watched from the front row as her mother practically glowed in an elegant ivory sheath dress, her hand clasped tightly in Bernard's as they sealed their union with a kiss.

Through the ceremony, Tanya felt Alexandre's presence across the aisle like a physical force. Each time the officiant mentioned love and destiny, their gazes would inadvertently meet, then dart away. The weight of their secret pressed heavily between them.

Tanya's heart swelled and sank in equal measure as she watched her mother and Bernard share that first kiss as husband and wife. Happiness radiated off Shaniece, a stark chatter of joy spilling over into the hushed crowd. The way her mother's eyes sparkled as she laughed at Bernard's whispered joke made Tanya's own heart ache with a strange blend of joy and apprehension.

From that day forward, everything was changing.

The lingering thought twisted her stomach. *How would she fit into this new family dynamic? She'd always enjoyed being the center of her mother's world. In many ways, it had shaped her. But now?* Would Shaniece still make time for deep talks over tea, or would those moments vanish into the ether as Bernard absorbed her undivided attention? Yes, Tanya could already see it; the new family bliss would crowd out their cherished mother-daughter moments.

She took a deep breath, forcing herself to focus on the ceremony, but her thoughts buzzed incessantly like dragonflies flitting around her head. What was she thinking? Selfishly resenting her mother's happiness? No. That wasn't who she was. She expanded her smile, grateful that her mother had found love in the twilight of her life. Bernard seemed kind and genuine, and Tanya could sense the connection between her mother and him.

But what about Alexandre?

Tanya's nerves tightened at the thought of him sitting so close, the two of them bound by a secret as heavy as an elephant in the room. Bernard would be part of the family now, her stepfather. And Alexandre would be... what? Her step-brother? That word felt surreal. The Frenchman she considered a one-night stand now belonged to her life in a way she never could have imagined.

What had started as an impulsive decision made during a whirlwind weekend in Paris had set her on a course she couldn't quite navigate. She stole a glance at Alexandre, still polished in a tailored suit, his blue eyes trained on the couple, but she could sense his awareness of her presence. An invisible thread tied them together, thick and electric, yet it was tangled with uncertainty.

Her own thoughts threatened to spiral out of control. What would happen if she told her mother? Would she be furious?

Disappointed? Would their tight bond unravel? Or would she accept that her daughter had willingly engaged in a night of passion—albeit with the man who now called her mother his wife's son? Tanya's throat dried as she wrestled with the weight of it all.

She began to feel perspiration bead on her brow despite the pleasant breeze. Why hadn't she kept it to herself? This could have been an uncomplicated affair, an adventure revealed only to the sleepy walls of her hotel room. But no, she was now tangled in the very fabric of her mother's new family.

As the officiant announced the end of the ceremony, she barely grasped the congratulatory smiles exchanged among the guests. Tanya's heart thudded in her chest, fear creeping through her like ivy overtaking a garden. *Would Alexandre see their shared history as scandalous or romantic? What did he think of her now that they were forced into this new hierarchy?*

"Don't overthink it," she muttered under her breath, summoning courage like a seasoned warrior.

But as the crowd began to disperse and the newlyweds floated away to greet their guests, Tanya found herself alone with her thoughts. She had wanted nothing more than to support her mother, to be genuinely happy for Shaniece. Yet now, a knot of anxiety clenched in her stomach.

She watched as Bernard pulled Shaniece into a tender embrace, their laughter echoing as they spun in playful circles. Her mother was so enamored, so in love. It should make Tanya feel warm inside, but the pang of unease twisted tighter. *How could she possibly disrupt this joyful moment?* She would be the one to spoil it, forever embedding herself into their memories like a pebble in a shoe.

And yet the truth loomed ahead like a dark cloud, unavoidable. Regret sat heavily on her shoulders, knowing she would either have to conceal her secret or unveil it in stark, unavoidable honesty. *But when? How could she time such a monumental revelation? Should she tell her mother tonight while the warmth and love hung palpably around them? Or should she wait?*

* * *

ALEXANDRE SHIFTED in his seat at the reception table, his champagne glass untouched. Across the sea of white linens and flower arrangements, Tanya sat beside her mother, her bronze skin glowing in the late afternoon sun. The way she tilted her head when she laughed made his chest tighten.

He'd never kept secrets from his father. Their relationship had always been built on trust and honesty, especially after his mother's death when Alexandre was twelve. Through those difficult years, Bernard had been both father and confidant, guiding Alexandre through grief while showing him how to become the man he was today.

His fingers drummed against the tablecloth as he watched his father lean over to whisper something in Shaniece's ear. The newlyweds radiated joy, their happiness infectious to everyone except him. How could he possibly disrupt their bliss with the truth about that night in Paris?

"You seem distracted, mon fils," Bernard called out, catching Alexandre's distant gaze.

Alexandre forced a smile. "Just taking it all in, Papa."

But his stomach churned with anxiety. The thought of family gatherings stretched before him like an endless maze - Christmas dinners where he'd have to pretend Tanya was just his step-sister, summer holidays at the villa where he'd watch her swim in the pool, knowing he couldn't touch her. Each scenario played out in his mind with increasing discomfort.

He loosened his tie slightly, feeling trapped by the formal wear and the weight of his thoughts. The band struck up another slow song, and couples drifted onto the dance floor. His father led Shaniece in a graceful waltz, their movements perfectly synchronized. They looked like they'd been dancing together for years instead of months.

A waiter passed by with fresh champagne, and Alexandre grabbed a glass, downing half of it in one gulp. The bubbles did nothing to settle his nerves. How was he supposed to maintain his composure around Tanya when every fiber of his being remembered the taste of her lips, the way her body had fit perfectly against his that night?

The memory of their passionate encounter clashed violently with the present reality. She wasn't just some beautiful stranger anymore - she was family now. His new step-sister. The thought made him want to laugh at the absurdity of it all, but the sound caught in his throat.

His eyes drifted back to Tanya, watching as she adjusted the strap of her bridesmaid's dress. That simple gesture sent his mind spinning back to their night together, when he'd traced that same shoulder with his fingers. He gripped his champagne glass tighter, his knuckles turning white.

Bernard had always taught him that honesty was paramount in any relationship. "A man's word is his bond," he'd say. But now, for the first time in his life, Alexandre found himself questioning whether the truth would do more harm than good. The revelation could shatter this newly formed family before it had a chance to truly begin.

His father's laughter carried across the reception space, deep and genuine. Alexandre couldn't remember the last time he'd heard that sound. After years of watching Bernard throw himself into work, using business as a shield against loneliness, his father had finally found happiness. Could Alexandre really risk destroying that?

A headache began to pulse behind his temples as he imagined the different ways this could play out. *Would his father be disappointed? Angry? Would he see it as a betrayal?* The questions swirled in his mind like the champagne in his glass, making him dizzy with uncertainty.

Meanwhile, Tanya sat there, impossibly beautiful and impossibly forbidden, a constant reminder of everything he couldn't have. The thought of seeing her at every family gathering, maintaining a polite distance while his body screamed to be closer, made him feel physically ill. He loosened his tie further, but it didn't help. The air felt thick and heavy, despite the perfect spring weather.

* * *

AT THE RECEPTION, strings of twinkling lights transformed the garden into an enchanted evening paradise. Champagne flowed freely as guests mingled on the stone terrace. Tanya noticed Alexandre speaking with his father near the fountain, their heads bent in serious conversation. Her stomach clenched when he caught her eye and gave a slight nod.

"Mama?" Tanya touched Shaniece's arm as she laughed with a group of Bernard's cousins. "Could we speak with you and Bernard for a moment? Privately?"

"Who is '*we*'?" Shaniece asked with a laugh in her voice.

Tanya dug her heel into the ground, "Alexandre and I."

Shaniece raised one eyebrow and and said, "Lead the way."

The four of them gathered in the library, its wood-paneled walls lined with leather-bound books. Bernard closed the heavy door behind them, muffling the sounds of celebration outside. Tanya perched on the edge of an antique settee while Alexandre remained standing, his hands pushed deep in his pockets.

"There's something we need to tell you," Alexandre began, his accent thicker with tension. "The night Tanya arrived in Paris..."

As they related their chance encounter and subsequent shock at discovering their connection, Tanya watched the color drain from her mother's face. Bernard's expression grew increasingly still, his jaw tightening. The silence that followed their confession stretched painfully.

Then Bernard let out a low chuckle. It started soft but grew until he was laughing openly, tears gathering at the corners of his eyes. Shaniece stared at him for a moment before joining in, her musical laughter filling the library.

"Oh honey," Shaniece wiped her eyes, reaching for Tanya's hand. "Did you really think we'd be angry? Love finds us in the most unexpected ways - look at Bernard and me."

"When I was your age," Bernard added, clapping Alexandre on the shoulder, "I spent a summer following a girl through every jazz club in New Orleans. The heart wants what it wants."

"But we are not in love," Alexandre blurted out, watching Tanya shoot him a weird look. His heart raced as the words left his mouth, feeling both true and somehow wrong at the same time.

"No," she added, "we're not." Tanya crossed her arms, trying to ignore the flutter in her stomach that suggested otherwise. The memory of their night together flickered through her mind, unbidden and unwanted.

Bernard and Shaniece embraced their children, then drifted back toward the party arm in arm, still chuckling and shaking their heads. The library door clicked shut behind them, leaving Tanya and Alexandre in weighted silence.

Their eyes lock and hold.

"Well, that went better than expected," Tanya said, smoothing her bridesmaid's dress. "But it doesn't change anything, does it?"

Alexandre shook his head slowly. "It's still... complicated. Our parents may accept it, but..."

"But we're step-siblings now," Tanya stood, needing to move. "It's too strange."

"Oui. You're right," he ran a hand through his hair. "Perhaps it's best if we..."

"Keep our distance," Tanya finished. "For everyone's sake."

They faced each other, the space between them charged with unspoken possibilities. Alexandre stepped forward and wrapped her in a tight embrace. Tanya pressed her face against his chest, breathing in his familiar scent one last time.

She lifted her head to say goodbye—but found his lips instead. The kiss deepened instantly, filled with all the passion and regret they couldn't voice. His hands tangled in her hair as she gripped his lapels, pulling him closer even as her mind screamed to let go.

Alexandre's fingers trembled against Tanya's neck as he deepened their kiss. Her soft moan vibrated through him, igniting every nerve ending. He traced her lower lip with his tongue, coaxing her mouth open, drowning in the taste of her. The sweetness of champagne mingled with something uniquely Tanya - a flavor that had haunted his dreams since that night in Paris.

Her hands slid up his chest, and he pressed closer, backing her against the library's mahogany shelves. Books shifted behind her as she arched into him. The solid weight of leather-bound volumes surrounded them, witnesses to this stolen moment. His thumb stroked the delicate skin beneath her ear while his other hand gripped her waist, holding her steady as he explored her mouth with increasing urgency.

The rest of the world dissolved. No wedding reception waiting outside. No complicated family dynamics. Just Tanya's breath mingling with his, her body soft and yielding against him. The familiar scent of her perfume - jasmine and vanilla - filled his senses, bringing back vivid memories of their night together. How perfectly they'd fit together then. How perfectly they fit now.

His heart hammered against his ribs as she tugged at his hair, drawing him even deeper into the kiss. Heat bloomed between them, and he could feel her pulse racing beneath his fingertips. Every touch, every taste reminded him why that single night had been impossible to forget. The connection between them crackled like lightning, electric and undeniable.

But reality crashed back when he tasted salt on his lips. Alexandre forced himself to pull away, though every cell in his body screamed in protest. His thumb caught a tear trailing down Tanya's cheek. More followed, leaving glistening tracks on her bronze skin.

The sight of her crying shattered something inside him. Her eyes, usually so bright and defiant, now shimmered with pain. Alexandre's chest constricted as he watched another tear fall, knowing he was partly responsible for her distress. The joy of kissing her twisted into an ache that settled deep in his bones.

"Au revoir, ma belle," he whispered, pressing his forehead to hers.

"Goodbye, Alexandre."

back to reality

. . .

Tanya

The Chicago skyline welcomed me back with its familiar steel and glass silhouette, but everything felt different. Empty. Wrong. The gallery that had been my sanctuary now felt like a prison of distractions that couldn't quite do their job.

I dove into work headfirst, scheduling back-to-back meetings with artists and collectors. My assistant Marcus raised his eyebrows at my suddenly packed calendar but knew better than to comment. The constant motion helped during daylight hours. It was the nights that killed me.

My Hyde Park condo, with its perfect view of Lake Michigan, became a torture chamber of memories. Every piece of art on my walls reminded me of conversations I'd imagined having with Alexandre about their meaning, their history. The French press in my kitchen mocked me – I hadn't touched it since returning from Paris.

"This is ridiculous," I muttered to myself, curled up on my couch with a glass of wine that tasted like ashes. "You barely knew him."

But that wasn't true. In that brief time, in that one night and those few precious days at his family's estate, I'd known him better than anyone I'd dated for months. The way his eyes crinkled when he smiled genuinely versus when he was being polite. How he absently ran his fingers through his hair when deep in thought. The sound of his laugh – God, his laugh.

I tried everything in my usual breakup arsenal. I queued up my favorite Netflix shows, but couldn't focus on a single plotline. The Hallmark Channel, my guilty pleasure during rough patches, just made me angry. Every predictable romance felt like a personal attack, a reminder that I'd walked away from something real.

My book collection gathered dust. I'd pick one up, read a paragraph, then find myself staring at the same words for minutes on end, my mind drifting to the way Alexandre had looked in the library of his family's estate. How natural he'd seemed there, surrounded by leather-bound volumes and history.

"Mama would know what to say," I whispered to my empty living room. But she was off enjoying her honeymoon with Bernard, and I couldn't bring myself to interrupt their happiness with my mess. Besides, what would I say? 'Hey Mama, remember how I told you I was fine with letting your stepson go? Well, I lied.'

The worst part was not knowing. Was he in Paris right now? Was he throwing himself into work like me? Did he sit in that beautiful library at night, thinking about me? Or had he already moved on, accepting our decision as the right one?

My pillow caught too many tears to count. Each night, I promised myself it would be the last time I cried over Alexandre Dubois. Each morning, I woke up with puffy eyes and a hollow chest that no amount of concealer could fix.

During one particularly low moment, I found myself googling flights to Paris. My finger hovered over the "Book Now" button before I slammed my laptop shut. That was a terrible idea. We'd made our choice. The fact that it felt like being stabbed in the heart every time I thought about it didn't change anything.

The gallery's newest exhibition – a collection of contemporary African American artists exploring themes of love and loss – felt like the universe laughing at me. Every piece spoke to my situation in ways I couldn't escape. A painting of two silhouettes reaching for each other across an impossible distance. A sculpture of intertwined hands breaking apart. An installation piece that played overlapping voice recordings in English and French.

At home, I couldn't even enjoy my usual evening run along the lakefront. The water reminded me of standing on that balcony in Paris, looking out over the Seine with Alexandre's warmth beside me. The summer breeze carried phantom traces of his cologne, and every tall man with dark hair made my heart skip before crushing disappointment set in.

My phone stayed suspiciously silent. No messages from Mama meant she was thoroughly enjoying her honeymoon, and I was glad for her happiness. But it also meant no news about Alexandre, no casual mentions of what he was doing or how he was handling our separation. The not knowing ate at me, corroding my carefully constructed walls of denial.

"These pieces need to be at least six inches apart," I directed the installation team, keeping my voice steady despite my exhaustion. "The artist specifically requested breathing room between each photograph."

Marcus appeared at my elbow with a steaming cup of coffee. "I added an extra shot of espresso. You look like you could use it."

"Is that your polite way of telling me I look terrible?" I accepted the cup, inhaling the rich aroma.

"I would never." He grinned, then struck an exaggerated pose next to one of the black and white portraits. "Though speaking of looking terrible, remember that time I tried to give myself highlights in college?"

Despite myself, I cracked a smile. Marcus had been my right hand at the gallery for three years, and he knew exactly how to lighten my mood. The memory of his orange-striped disaster still made me laugh.

"There she is." His expression softened. "I was starting to worry we'd lost you to whatever's been eating you up these past weeks."

I turned away, pretending to study the spacing between photographs. "I don't know what you're talking about."

"Please." He gestured for the installation team to take a break, then guided me toward my office. "You've been walking around like someone stole your favorite Basquiat. And don't think I haven't noticed you've been wearing the same three outfits on rotation."

"I've been busy," I protested weakly as he closed my office door.

"Tanya Michelle Washington, I have watched you pull off simultaneous gallery openings while planning your mother's birthday gala without breaking a sweat." He perched on the edge of my desk. "This is different. This is about a man."

The words stuck in my throat. I hadn't told anyone about Alexandre, about our impossible situation. But Marcus's concerned expression broke something loose inside me.

"I met someone in Paris," I whispered. "Before the wedding. Before I knew who he was."

Marcus leaned forward. "Who he was?"

"My new stepbrother." The words tasted bitter. I told him everything – the magical night at the wine bar, the shock of recognition at the wedding, our painful decision to walk away.

"Girl." Marcus shook his head slowly. "You're really out here living a whole romance novel."

"It's not funny," I said, but a hysterical laugh bubbled up anyway.

"No, it's not." He took my hands in his. "It's tragic. And you're both idiots."

"Excuse me?"

"You heard me. You're in love with him."

"I barely know him," I protested.

"But you *want* to know him. And he clearly feels the same way, or you wouldn't both be so torn up about walking away." He squeezed my hands. "So why are you still here?"

"Because..." I trailed off, realizing I didn't have a good answer. "It's complicated."

"Life is complicated. Love is complicated. But you know what's simple? Getting on a plane." He pulled out his phone. "Let's check flights right now."

"Marcus, I can't just—"

"Yes, you can. Look, your mother married a man she'd known for five minutes because she recognized something real. Maybe it's time you took a page from her book."

My chest felt lighter than it had in weeks. The possibility I'd been denying myself suddenly seemed within reach.

"There's a direct flight tomorrow morning," Marcus said, still scrolling. "First class is available. Should I book it for you?"

I thought about Alexandre's blue eyes, about the way he'd looked at me that last time in the library. About all the things we'd left unsaid.

That kiss. God, that kiss in the library haunted my dreams and my waking hours. The way Alexandre's hands had framed my face, how his lips claimed mine with equal parts desperation and tenderness. The memory of his touch sent electricity coursing through my body, making my skin tingle and my heart race.

Every night, I'd sink into my oversized tub, trying to wash away thoughts of him. But the hot water only intensified the memories – his fingers trailing down my spine, his breath hot against my neck, the solid warmth of his chest pressed against mine. I'd close my eyes and be right back there in that Parisian hotel room, lost in the symphony of sighs and whispered French endearments.

My fingers traced my lips, remembering how perfectly his mouth fit against mine. The library kiss had been different from our first night together – deeper, more meaningful. Like he'd been trying to memorize every sensation, every taste. Like he'd known it would be our last.

"Dammit." I pressed my palms against my eyes, fighting back tears. *Who was I kidding?* This wasn't just sexual attraction or chemistry. This was something else entirely. Something that made my chest ache and my breath catch whenever I thought about him.

I missed his voice, the way it got slightly deeper when he was serious about something. I missed his laugh – that genuine, unguarded sound that came straight from his soul. I missed how he'd run his fingers through his hair when he was thinking hard about something, leaving it adorably mussed.

Even the little things tortured me. The way he took his coffee (black, no sugar). How he always touched my lower back when we walked through doorways. The slight accent that crept into his perfect English when he was tired or emotional.

"What am I doing?" I whispered under my breath. Here I was, wallowing in memories while Marcus waited for my answer about the flight. What exactly was I waiting for? Permission? From who? The universe had already thrown us together in the most impossible way – maybe that was all the sign I needed.

I thought about my mother, how brave she'd been in following her heart. She'd taught me to be strong, independent, cautious. But she'd also shown me that sometimes the biggest risks led to the greatest rewards.

"Time's ticking, boss lady. These first-class seats won't wait forever."

The thought of seeing Alexandre again made my heart hammer against my ribs. What if he'd moved on? What if he thought I wasn't worth the complications? What if...

No. No more what-ifs. I was done letting fear make my decisions.

"Book it."

retour à la normale

...

Alexandre

The Paris skyline blurred past my car window as Pierre, my driver, navigated through morning traffic. Another day at the office. Another attempt at normalcy. But who was I kidding? Nothing felt normal anymore.

I scrolled through acquisition proposals on my tablet, the words swimming before my eyes. My mind drifted to Tanya's face, the way her eyes had glistened when we'd said goodbye in the library. The memory hit me like a physical ache in my chest.

"Monsieur Dubois?" My assistant Charlotte's voice snapped me back to reality. "Your nine o'clock is waiting."

Right. Work. Focus. I straightened my tie and strode into the conference room, where potential investors waited to discuss our latest sustainable housing project. Usually, these meetings energized me. Today, I merely went through the motions.

Hours blended together. Meetings. Calls. Endless emails. I buried myself in spreadsheets and environmental impact reports until my eyes burned. But every quiet moment betrayed me. In the reflection of my office windows, I saw Tanya's smile. In the buzz of my phone, I hoped for a message that wouldn't come.

That evening, my apartment felt emptier than ever. I turned on the PSG match, hoping football would provide its usual escape. But even as Mbappé scored a brilliant goal, my thoughts wandered to Tanya. Would she have enjoyed watching with me? Would she have teased me about my passionate support for Paris Saint-Germain?

"Merde," I muttered, switching off the TV. Even Jean and Marc's invitation to a jazz concert at Le Petit Journal couldn't shake this melancholy. The music was excellent, the crowd electric, but I felt disconnected from it all. My friends noticed.

"What's wrong with you lately?" Jean asked during intermission. "You look like someone killed your dog."

I forced a laugh. "Just tired. Work's been intense."

But lying in bed that night, sleep eluded me again. The city lights cast shadows across my ceiling as questions tormented me. Was she having trouble sleeping too? Was she thinking about our kiss? About what could have been?

I reached for my phone, thumbing through news articles about Chicago's art scene, searching for any mention of her gallery. Pathetic. I knew it was pathetic. But I couldn't help myself.

Father would know how she was doing - or at least how Shaniece was doing, which might give me some insight. But he and Shaniece were somewhere in the Maldives, probably sipping cocktails on a beach, blissfully unaware of my internal struggle.

My workout routine, usually a reliable stress reliever, felt hollow. Even swimming laps in my building's pool - typically my meditation time - became an exercise in frustration. The rhythmic strokes couldn't drown out thoughts of her laugh, her wit, the way she'd challenged my perspectives during our conversations.

Work became my refuge and my prison. I tackled projects with aggressive focus, staying late into the evening. Charlotte started leaving concerned Post-it notes on my desk about "work-life balance." But what was waiting for me at home except memories and regret?

My friends tried their best. They dragged me to matches, concerts, wine tastings - all the things I usually loved. But everything felt muted, like watching life through frosted glass. During a particularly good set at the jazz club, I caught myself composing texts to Tanya in my head, sharing observations I knew she'd appreciate.

The worst part? The irony of it all. I'd spent years building walls around my heart, focusing on work, keeping relationships casual. Then one night with her had shattered everything. Now, trying to rebuild those walls felt impossible - and honestly, I wasn't sure I wanted to.

I found myself walking past the wine bar where we'd met, torturing myself with memories of that first electric connection. How could something that felt so right be wrong just because of circumstance? The question haunted me, keeping me awake as Paris slept.

* * *

I STARED at the projections on my monitor, but the numbers blurred together. Another sleepless night left me running on espresso and determination.

"Your coffee, monsieur." Charlotte swept into my office with fresh espresso and a knowing smile. "And these contracts need your signature." She placed them on my desk with exaggerated formality, then struck a pose. "Shall I fetch your slippers and pipe as well, oh great one?"

Her antics usually made me laugh, but today I could barely muster a weak smile. "Merci, Charlotte."

She didn't leave. Instead, she perched on the edge of my desk, arms crossed. "That's it. I've watched you mope around this office for weeks. You're not fooling anyone, Alexandre."

"I'm not moping." I shuffled papers, avoiding her gaze. "I'm focused."

"Please. You look like someone ran over your puppy. Multiple times." She leaned forward. "What happened in Chicago?"

My head snapped up. "What makes you think—"

"You've been checking flight schedules to O'Hare. Your browser history is full of Chicago art galleries. And you keep staring at that awful modernist print like it holds the secrets of the universe."

I glanced at the piece in question - a bold abstract I'd purchased from Tanya's gallery before leaving Chicago. "It's not awful."

"It looks like someone sneezed paint onto canvas." Charlotte's expression softened. "Talk to me, Alexandre. We've worked together for five years. I know when something's eating at you."

The weight of keeping everything inside suddenly felt unbearable. "I met someone." The words tumbled out. "In Paris, before my father's wedding. She was... extraordinary. Smart. Challenging. Beautiful." I ran a hand through my hair. "And then I discovered she was my new stepsister."

Charlotte's eyes widened. "Mon Dieu."

"We agreed it was too complicated. That we should go our separate ways." I stood, pacing to the window. "It was the rational decision."

"And how's that working out for you?"

I pressed my forehead against the cool glass. "Terribly."

"Then what are you doing here?"

I sat back down. "Running a multinational company? Being responsible? Not complicating my father's marriage?"

Charlotte made a disgusted sound. "You're being an idiot." She spun my chair around to face her. "Life is messy, Alexandre. Love is messy. If you've found someone who makes your world stop spinning, you fight for that. You don't hide in your office pretending spreadsheets can fill the void in your heart."

"But—"

"No buts. Get on a plane. Go to Chicago. Tell her you were wrong." She pulled up my calendar on her tablet. "You have no critical meetings this week. I can reschedule everything else."

"Charlotte—"

"Do you love her?"

Charlotte's question echoed in my mind. Did I love Tanya?

I swiveled away from her penetrating gaze, staring out at the Paris skyline without really seeing it. Love seemed too simple a word for this constant ache in my chest, this endless loop of memories playing in my head.

Every morning, I woke reaching for my phone, hoping to see her name. During meetings, I caught myself sketching her profile in the margins of my notes - the curve of her cheek, the arch of her eyebrow when she was skeptical about something I'd said. Even now, weeks later, I could still feel the phantom warmth of her hand in mine as we'd sat on those limestone steps.

"Alexandre?" Charlotte's voice cut through my reverie. "You haven't answered my question."

How could I explain that Tanya had somehow worked her way into every corner of my life? That I found myself collecting stories I wanted to share with her, jokes that would make her laugh, observations about art that would spark one of our spirited debates?

The coffee shop near my apartment had started making me think of her - she'd mentioned loving their pain au chocolat during one of our conversations at the wedding. I'd actually bought two yesterday morning before remembering she wasn't here to share them with.

"I keep a running list," I admitted quietly, more to myself than Charlotte. "Of things I want to tell her. Places in Paris I want to show her. Arguments I want to have with her about modern art versus classical. It's pathetic, really."

My nights had become an exercise in restraint, stopping myself from booking flights to Chicago on impulse. During particularly weak moments, I'd found myself looking up her gallery's website, reading press releases about upcoming exhibitions just to feel some connection to her world.

The worst part? The little things. How a certain shade of amber in my evening whiskey reminded me of her eyes. The way I'd catch myself turning to share a thought with someone who wasn't there. Even my morning runs through Luxembourg Gardens had become bittersweet - I couldn't help imagining her beside me, her locs bouncing with each stride, challenging me to keep up.

"I dream about her," I confessed, still facing the window. "Not just at night. Daydreams. Random moments when I should be focused on work or meetings. I'll see something beautiful or interesting, and my first thought is always of sharing it with her."

My fingers traced patterns on the glass. "Yesterday, I found myself in a heated debate with Tomas about sustainable urban development - one of my passion projects. All I could think about was how Tanya would have loved jumping into that conversation, challenging both our perspectives with her unique viewpoint."

The memory of our last kiss haunted me - the way she'd melted into my arms, the taste of her tears mixing with mine. We'd agreed it was for the best, but every fiber of my being screamed that we were wrong.

"When she's not here, everything feels... muted somehow. Like Paris has lost some of its vibrancy." I turned back to Charlotte. "Is that love? This constant awareness of absence? This feeling that everything I experience is somehow incomplete because I can't share it with her?"

I thought about how naturally she'd fit into my world during those brief days we'd had together. How her presence had made everything sharper, more vivid. How her challenges to my ideas had pushed me to think differently, to see things from new angles.

"I find myself buying books I think she'd enjoy, marking passages I want to discuss with her. I've started following Chicago news, just to feel closer to her world." I ran a hand through my hair in frustration. "I even caught myself researching Chicago's art scene, contemplating opening a branch office there just to have an excuse to visit."

The weight of these feelings pressed against my chest. Was this love? This constant orbit around thoughts of her? This persistent ache of wanting to be near her, to hear her laugh, to watch her eyes light up during our debates?

Or was it just the allure of forbidden fruit? The human tendency to want what we couldn't have?

The question hit me like a physical blow. "Yes," I whispered, finally admitting it aloud.

"Then stop making excuses." She was already typing on her tablet. "I'm booking you on the first flight tomorrow morning."

Something shifted in my chest - like a weight lifting, a door opening. The anxiety that had been my constant companion these past weeks transformed into anticipation.

"What about the Goldman proposal?" I asked weakly.

"I'll handle it." She waved dismissively. "Pack a bag. Get some sleep. Your car will pick you up at five."

I caught her arm as she headed for the door. "Thank you, Charlotte."

She smiled. "Just promise me one thing - when this works out, you'll replace that hideous painting with something that doesn't look like a colorblind toddler's tantrum."

For the first time in weeks, I laughed genuinely. Opening my laptop, I pulled up my travel documents. The familiar rush of planning, of taking action, energized me. Chicago. Tanya. No more hiding behind practicality and obligation.

I spent the next hour making arrangements, my mind already racing ahead to what I would say, how I would convince her that some things were worth fighting for. Charlotte popped her head in occasionally, confirming details and giving me a thumbs up.

By the time I left the office that evening, my ticket was booked, my schedule cleared. The Paris evening felt different somehow - full of possibility rather than regret. Tomorrow morning, I would board a plane to Chicago and finally do what I should have done weeks ago - follow my heart.

epilogue
. . .

*A*lexandre did not want to wait until morning to catch a flight and booked an overnight to Chicago.

He dragged his carry-on through O'Hare's Terminal 5, his body heavy with jetlag and his heart heavier with regret. The fluorescent lights cast harsh shadows across the faces of travelers rushing past him. He'd fallen into a daze, letting muscle memory guide him toward baggage claim, when a flash of familiar curly locs caught his attention.

His steps faltered. Logic told him it couldn't be her - what were the odds? But his heart recognized her silhouette before his mind could process it. Tanya stood near the check-in counter, her cream blazer a beacon among the crowd of rushing travelers.

Across the terminal, Tanya's fingers tightened around her boarding pass as she spotted a tall figure in a perfectly tailored navy suit. Her breath caught. The way he moved, that subtle confidence - it had to be Alexandre. She blinked hard, convinced her mind was playing tricks on her after too many sleepless nights.

But when she opened her eyes, he was still there. Their gazes connected across the sea of travelers, and the bustling airport seemed to freeze around them.

Alexandre's pulse quickened. He'd rehearsed a thousand speeches on the flight over, but now, seeing her, words failed him. His feet refused to move, caught between the magnetic pull toward her and the memory of their tearful goodbye.

Tanya's legs trembled as she took the first step forward. Then another. The crowd parted around her like a stream around a stone as she made her way toward him, her heels clicking against the polished floor.

They came to stand before each other, close enough to touch but separated by an invisible wall of uncertainty. The air crackled between them with unspoken words and untamed desire.

Alexandre's blue eyes searched her face, drinking in every detail he'd tried so hard to forget. The subtle arch of her eyebrows, the fullness of her lips, the way her amber eyes sparked with recognition and something deeper.

"I couldn't stay away," Tanya whispered, her voice barely audible above the airport announcements. "I was flying to Paris. To find you." Her hands trembled as she reached for him, stopping just short of touching his chest.

"And I couldn't let you go," Alexandre replied, his French accent thicker with emotion. "I flew to Chicago. For you."

The confession hung between them like a tangible thing. Tanya's carefully constructed walls began to crack, emotion flooding through. "I tried to forget you. To convince myself it was impossible. But everything reminds me of you. The way you look at me, the way you make me feel..." Her voice cracked with vulnerability.

Epilogue

Alexandre stepped closer, close enough to catch the subtle scent of her jasmine perfume. "I threw myself into work, into distractions. Nothing helped. You're in my thoughts constantly. When I close my eyes, I see your smile. When I open them, I look for you in every crowd."

Their bodies collided with magnetic force, erasing the careful distance they'd tried to maintain. Tanya's arms wrapped around Alexandre's back, her fingers clutching the fine wool of his suit jacket as if he might disappear if she loosened her grip. His own arms encircled her waist, pulling her closer until the rapid beating of their hearts seemed to synchronize.

The bustling airport faded into white noise around them. A luggage cart squeaked past. Someone's phone chimed. An announcement echoed through the terminal. But in their bubble of connection, these sounds barely registered.

Alexandre breathed in the familiar scent of her hair, allowing himself to acknowledge how much he'd missed her. The emptiness that had plagued him since their goodbye dissolved with her warmth pressed against him. Her small frame fit perfectly against his chest, exactly as he remembered.

Tanya pressed her face into his shoulder, inhaling the subtle notes of his cologne that had haunted her dreams. Tears pricked at her eyes as the reality of their reunion settled over her. The universe had conspired to bring them together, their hearts pulling them across an ocean to the same spot at the same moment.

"I can't believe you're here," she murmured against his chest, her voice thick with emotion. She felt his arms tighten around her in response, his cheek resting against the top of her head.

The solid warmth of his body grounded her, making the past weeks of sleepless nights and distracted days feel like a distant dream. His heartbeat thundered under her ear, strong and steady, matching the rapid tempo of her own.

Alexandre's hands splayed across her back, memorizing the feel of her in his arms. The cream fabric of her blazer bunched beneath his fingers as he held her closer. He'd imagined this moment countless times during lonely nights in his Paris apartment, but reality far surpassed his fantasies.

Their embrace drew curious glances from passing travelers, but neither noticed. They remained locked together, swaying slightly as if moved by music only they could hear. The synchronicity of their breathing, the perfect fit of their bodies, the electric current of connection flowing between them - it all felt meant to be.

Tanya's fingers traced small circles on Alexandre's back, reassuring herself that he was real, that this wasn't another dream she'd wake from alone in her Chicago apartment. The solid muscle beneath her hands, the subtle tremor that ran through him at her touch, the steady rise and fall of his chest - these sensations anchored her in the moment.

His cologne wrapped around her like a familiar blanket, bringing back vivid memories of their night in Paris. But this was different. This wasn't a fleeting encounter or a goodbye embrace. This felt like coming home.

Alexandre marveled at how perfectly she molded against him, as if they'd been designed as two parts of the same whole. Her curves fit his angles, her softness complemented his strength. The ghost of emptiness that had haunted him since their parting finally ceased its relentless ache.

Time seemed to stretch and compress around them. Seconds or hours might have passed as they stood wrapped in each other's arms. The rest of the world continued its frantic pace while they remained still, existing in a pocket of space where only their connection mattered.

Her warmth seeped through his clothes, chasing away the chill of lonely nights and hollow days. The subtle floral notes of her perfume mixed with her natural scent, creating an intoxicating combination that made him lightheaded with joy.

Their hearts continued their synchronized dance, beating out a rhythm of reunion and recognition. The universe had orchestrated this impossible meeting, bringing them together across miles and time zones to this exact moment. Neither was willing to loosen their grip, afraid the magic might shatter if they let go.

* * *

A YEAR LATER

The grand ballroom of Le Meurice sparkled with champagne flutes and laughter as hundreds of Paris's elite gathered to celebrate Bernard and Shaniece Dubois's first wedding anniversary. Crystal chandeliers cast a warm glow over the elegant crowd, their light catching on jewels and cufflinks as guests mingled beneath gilded ceilings.

Shaniece radiated joy in a flowing emerald gown, her hand never leaving Bernard's as they greeted their guests. The past year had transformed them both - her natural vivacity now enhanced by the contentment of deep love, his aristocratic bearing softened by genuine happiness.

Tanya watched her mother from across the room, marveling at how naturally Shaniece had adapted to Parisian high society while maintaining her authentic self. The way Bernard looked at her mother still made Tanya's heart swell - that same expression of wonder and devotion he'd worn on their wedding day.

"Your mother has revolutionized how we do business," Alexandre murmured in her ear, sliding an arm around her waist. "Papa says her marketing expertise has doubled our sustainable housing projects' visibility."

Tanya leaned into her husband's embrace, remembering how different things had felt at last year's wedding. The panic, the guilt, the bittersweet resignation of their goodbye - all of it washed away by that chance encounter at O'Hare Airport three days later.

"Remember how you nearly knocked over that poor businessman when you saw me at my gate?" she teased, turning to face him.

"I maintain he was in my way." Alexandre's blue eyes crinkled with amusement. "Though I'd have knocked over the entire airport to reach you."

They had abandoned their flights that day, racing to the nearest courthouse instead. The judge had raised her eyebrows at their breathless explanation, but something in their desperate certainty must have convinced her. Within hours, they had exchanged simple vows and silver rings from a nearby jewelry shop.

"Your father's face when we called him on his honeymoon to tell him," Tanya laughed softly. "I thought he was going to drop the phone."

"Mama just said 'finally' and demanded photos," Alexandre recalled, pulling her closer as the orchestra struck up a slow waltz. Their parents had cut short their Mediterranean cruise to throw an impromptu celebration dinner, where Bernard had proudly declared that fate clearly had a better plan than any of them.

Epilogue

Across the ballroom, Bernard now spun Shaniece in a perfect waltz, her emerald skirts swirling as other couples joined them on the dance floor. The sight of their parents' happiness had become a constant reminder that love could thrive in the most unexpected circumstances.

"I never thought I'd find this," Tanya admitted, resting her head against Alexandre's chest as they swayed to the music. "Someone who feels like home, no matter which side of the ocean we're on."

Alexandre pressed a kiss to her temple. "You changed everything. My whole life was perfectly ordered until you crashed into it. Now I can't imagine going back to that kind of control."

Tanya lifted her face to his, heart full of the same overwhelming love she'd felt that day in the airport. "I love you."

"Je t'aime aussi, mon coeur," Alexandre murmured, drawing her into a passionate kiss that made several nearby couples clear their throats pointedly.

THE END

you might also like

love child - part 1

Trixi Matthews had always known who her biological father was. Her mother had been a maid in the wealthy businessman's household for years, and Mr. Fischer frequently took advantage of her mother's youth.

Twenty-four years later, Trixi now wants to know him. At first, stalking Mr. Fischer had been easy - she had easily gone unnoticed until she's discovered by the covert operations of his wayward son.

Grayson Fischer had noticed her from the start! Trixi was unlike any girl he'd ever seen - but who was she really?

They meet by chance, and Trixi keeps her secret … until Grayson begins to show his feelings for her. Find out what happens when the mystery gets revealed.

Part 1 of 2

BWWM Romance

Ebook & Paperback

love child - part 2

Grayson Fischer cannot believe his horrible fate. He's found the woman of his dreams—but she turns out to be his half-sister? What hellish nightmare was this?

Trixi Matthews finally gets to know her biological father, it's all she's ever dreamed of, but her feelings for Grayson make her lovesick with the understanding of the truth.

What happens to Trixi and Grayson? Do they give into their twisted attraction to one another? Or do they go their separate ways, and face eternal heartbreak?

Find out what happens in Part Two of "Love Child - A BWWM Romance"

Part 2 of 2

A BWWM Romance

Ebook & Paperback

new for 2025

dorm room 2b or not 2b

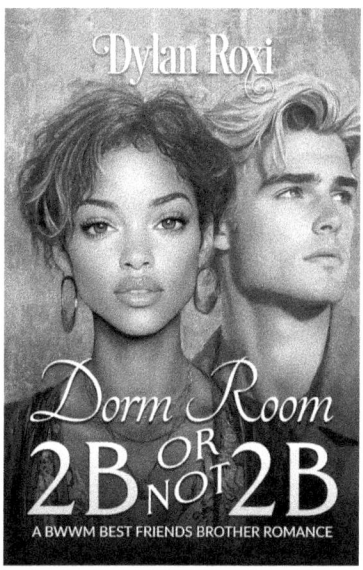

from enemies to lovers, this sizzling romance will have you swooning!

Whitney Barnes, a whirlwind of talent and sass, knows how to navigate the chaos of college theater. But her world is thrown into disarray when her roommate's infuriatingly handsome brother, David, moves in. Once the bane of her teenage sleepovers, he's now a brooding film student with a camera that seems to always be on her.

As they embark on a documentary project capturing the vibrant underground arts scene, an unexpected connection ignites. Late-night editing sessions, sunrise coffee runs, and shared secrets blur the lines between friendship and something more. Whitney must decide if she's ready to step out of character and embrace the unpredictable, messy, and undeniably captivating reality of falling for her best friend's brother.

A BWWM Best Friends Brother Romance

Available in

Ebook & Paperback

about dylan

Dylan Roxi is an emerging author of BWWM Romance and Contemporary Modern Fiction. Dylan has many writing interests and lives an incognito digital lifestyle.

Dylan is part of the Ardent Artist Books family and is the author of several published books.

> amazon.com/Ardent-Artist-Books/e/B08BX8F1DZ
> youtube.com/theardentartist

also by dylan

Love Child - Part 1

Love Child - Part 2

Offsides

Almost Yours

Cougar at Play

Paris Fling

Dorm Room 2B or Not 2B

www.ingramcontent.com/pod-product-compliance
Lightning Source LLC
LaVergne TN
LVHW021828060526
838201LV00058B/3560